Edward Sylvester Ellis

Monowano, the Shawnee Spy

Edward Sylvester Ellis

Monowano, the Shawnee Spy

ISBN/EAN: 9783337299415

Printed in Europe, USA, Canada, Australia, Japan

Cover: Foto ©Andreas Hilbeck / pixelio.de

More available books at **www.hansebooks.com**

MONOWANO;

THE SHAWNEE SPY.

LONDON:

GEORGE ROUTLEDGE AND SONS,

THE BROADWAY, LUDGATE.

PUBLISHERS' NOTE.

In this romance of "the Dark and Bloody Ground"—as Kentucky is baptized in her early history—the reader is introduced once more to the inimitable Peter Jenkins, and Dick Dingle the ranger, whose appearance in "The Frontier Angel" added so much to the interest of that popular and enticing romance. They will be welcomed, for their part now is that of principals: and their singular characters, their adventures in the celebrated Nickajack Expedition and in the rescue of the Mordaunt party, their relations to the Spy of the story, all serve to render the Trail Hunters men to be remembered.

THE SHAWNEE SPY.

CHAPTER I

THE TRAIL-HUNTERS

"I CAN'T see the use of the Injins acting so mean all the time. They're always trying to rob and kill the people along the frontier; and if a fellow like me undertakes to go into *their* country to look at things, he's sure to get chased out again, and ef he happens to get catched they won't take any apology or excuse, but court-martial him on the spot. Confound them! it's time they learned better."

The speaker was Peter Jenkins, who, while uttering the above remarks, was coiled up in the branches of a luxuriant oak, where he deemed even the gleaming eye of a Shawnee could not reach him. For miles around stretched the wilds of Western Kentucky, swarming with Indians and wild beasts, with here and there a solitary block-house or settlement. The time was in the early summer of 1794, a short period previous to the celebrated battle and treaty of Wayne.

It would have been almost impossible to discover the hiding-place of Jenkins. He had been ranging through the country for the past week, and was now returning homeward To avoid pursuit, he had concealed his trail as much as possible, and had spent the night in the tree as the most certain retreat from discovery. He had but just awakened and was communing with himself. Peter was a long, gaunt personage, with dangling feet and arms, and yet, withal, a person of uncommon activity. His face was homely, but expressive of good-humor and frankness. He had large, innocent blue eyes, a huge nose, and irregular features. His costume was the same as that worn by the hunters of the day, consisting of the usual leggins, hunting-shirt, etc.

"It *is* strange how them Injins will go on; they're all the time up to some deviltry. Shouldn't wonder at all if there's a lot following me. If there don't too many come, I don't care. When I first come out here, I own I was somewhat skeerish; but I'm getting over that, though there *is* something about the painted imps that always makes me feel nervous. Dingle has cured me of the fear I used to have, though now and then them fainting fits will come over me, just when they shouldn't. Well, well, I suppose—hello! who shot that!"

The last exclamation had good cause for its utterance; for the report of a rifle, a few rods away, was followed by the sharp cutting of a bullet through the leaves, within almost a hair's breadth of Jenkins' head. The startled trail-hunter nervously ducked his head, and shrunk still closer to the limb of the tree upon which he had ensconced himself.

"That's mean, by thunder! to treat a fellow that way!" he indignantly exclaimed to himself. "S'pose I'm hit with a bullet, just see what a fall I must have! It would break my neck as sure as the world! Now, Pete Jenkins, bring your biggest powers into play."

As he uttered these words, he extended himself in a horizontal position upon the limb, and skillfully worked his way toward the trunk of the tree.

When he reached this he glided as dextrously as a squirrel to the opposite side from which the shot came, where, humping himself up like a coon, he settled down into the hollow formed by the insertion of a huge limb, and carefully listened.

For nearly an hour, not the slightest sound betrayed the presence of a foe. At the end of that time, he detected the crackling of a twig, as though made by the cautious passage of a person. He strained himself to the utmost to catch a glimpse of his enemy, but the dense foliage of the oak prevented.

"You can hunt around in the bushes there as long as you're a mind to, so you don't get another crack at me. If I can only draw bead on your ugly picture once, you'll be sorry that you ever waked up Peter Jenkins. He is a dangerous man when he is once aroused."

Again the speaker ducked his head, for a bullet gouged the limb upon which he was sitting, and glancing upward, shot out into mid-air, with that peculiar *zip-zip*, made by the passage of a bullet through the foliage of a tree. This second shot so alarmed Jenkins that he nestled still closer to the trunk, hardly daring to even whisper to himself. A half-hour of silence, disturbed only by the distant cawing of a crow, passed away without further incident. Jenkins, gathering courage from the long silence, began to peer cautiously downward, circling his head like the bewildered serpent. Through the interstices of the leaves, he suddenly distinguished two small, starlike eyes, gleaming like a basilisk's from the undergrowth, and fixed with an intense brightness upon himself.

"What infarnal looking eyes! They shine exactly like Tecumseh's," exclaimed Jenkins, gliding hurriedly to the opposite side of the tree. Here he ensconced himself as securely as circumstances would permit, and again sought for the hiding-place of his enemy. He discovered it instantly, the orbs still fixed, and scintillating with a frightful gleaming.

"If you haven't got more manners than to look at a fellow, like that, I'll teach you," said Jenkins, reaching and feeling above him for his rifle, which he had laid across a couple of limbs. As his hand rested on the stock, a jet of fire flamed from the hiding-place of his enemy, and at the same instant a jar shook the rifle in his hand so suddenly, and with such a singular, stunning effect, as to unloose his grasp and cause the weapon to fall end over end through the limbs to the ground.

"Well there! that was well done, if it was a redskin that done it. You hit the barrel with your bullet and knocked my gun clean out of my hand before I could use it. The next shot I s'pose will serve me the same way."

If such was Jenkins' expectation, he did his utmost to avoid it, for he ascended still further and concealed himself still more. While gazing in the direction where he judged his enemy to be concealed, the forest again rung with the sharp echo of the latter's rifle, and the messenger of death whistled so close to the trail-hunter's face, that for an instant he believed he was shot. A moment more, however, showed that he was entirely unharmed.

It was now obvious to Jenkins that whoever had fired at
him had purposely missed him. A marksman who had evince
such remarkable skill could not have failed so often.
required but a moment for Jenkins to satisfy himself of th
meaning of all this. It was a direct summons to surrende
and, in his present defenseless state, much as he regretted i
there was no alternative. He reflected a moment, and the
called out :

"Halloa, you, down there, don't shoot any more. I com
to terms! I surrender, for it can't be helped. But I war
you to understand it's a *conditional* surrender. My rights al
to be respected, my property preserved, and personal safet
sworn to. There mustn't be any tomahawks, or knives, o
such things in circulation. If these conditions are submitte
to, I *descend*."

He did not wait to receive the reply of his captor, but cor
menced descending with a wonderful celerity and readines
In a few moments he dropped lightly to the ground, an
looked around for his enemy. But no one was to be seer
Jenkins' eyes kindled as he beheld his rifle lying upon th
ground a few yards away, and he instantly resolved to recove
it, and reconsider his "conditional surrender." He glanced fur
tively around, and detecting no signs of his foe, stepped hur
riedly toward the coveted object. Instantly a deep, rumblin
voice commanded :

"Stop!"

Jenkins felt his hair fairly rise on end at the startling com
mand. He wheeled around but still failed to see the speaker
Vexation, in part at the whimsical orders to which he wa
submitting, now took the place of his fear, and he exclaimed

"Why don't you show yourself, whoever you are? S'pos
you're afraid, the way you're sneaking around. Come ou
here like a man, and I'll talk over matters with you."

Jenkins fairly sprung in the air as a low, familiar, taunting
laugh reached his ears. At that moment he would have
rather heard the war-whoop of Tecumseh and encountered
him in a hand-to-hand struggle, than have met the man in
whose presence he now stood.

"I know who you are. Come out here."

The next moment the undergrowth parted, and a large
powerfully formed hunter stepped into view.

"How are you, Dingle? Glad to see you!" said Jenkins, stepping forward, and offering his hand.

The person addressed, instead of accepting the proffered hand, placed his own against his side, and, without speaking, looked in Jenkins' face with a faint, tantalizing smile. The latter, disconcerted and vexed, said:

"If you're too proud to shake hands, I don't care! I'm as good as you are. I can get along without you, I guess!"

"It's a 'conditional surrender,'" said Dingle, without stirring.

"No it isn't, either!" replied Jenkins, catching up his rifle.

"What do you mean?" demanded Dingle, his brow lowering like a thunder-cloud.

Jenkins threw his gun over his shoulder, and, in turn, asked:

"What do *you* mean, Dick?"

"Jenkins, you're a pretty good fellow," said Dingle, without heeding the question. "When you first come in these parts you was powerful afraid of the redskins. Ever since that time I've been trying to cure you of it. I don't believe you're as *nervous* now as you was then, but you've got too much of that thing about you yet."

"What would you have done, Dick, in my place?"

"Sot still and got shot, before I'd 'ave come down for a red. I don't know though, Jenkins; you're improving, I think. You was in a bad fix, and you done the best you could. I jest shot to see how you would act. I didn't expect you'd try to shoot me as you did. Yes, Peter, I'm thinking you'll be somethin' one of these days."

"It seems to me it was rather a foolish thing in you, Dingle, to fire when you didn't know but what it would bring down a whole pack of the dogs upon you."

"Dingle *did* know all about that," significantly replied the latter. "I've been beating all around this neighborhood for the last day or two, and the only trail within ten miles of here is yours and mine. Where have you been?"

"Up the Sciota Valley, taking observations on the Shawnee towns."

"What did you see?"

"Nothing uncommon. Things are about the same. They

are painting, and yelling, and flinging the tomahawk the same as ever, but I couldn't make out exactly what they intended to do. Have they been up to any of their capers in these parts while I was gone ?"

"Not exactly in these parts, but they've raised thunder down in Tennessee. A whole pack have been tearing through the country, burning houses, blowing up flat-boats, and making a general wiping out."

"Why don't the people rise up in their wrath and devour them ?"

"There ain't enough whites in them regions, and they've sent up several runners axing us to help 'em pitch into the varmints."

"Is it going to be done ?"

"Going to be done ? In *course* it is !"

"Who's going to do it ?"

"They've axed old Captain Bill Whitley to scare up a hundred boys and bring 'em down. I've promised him that me and you will go, and he has sot down our names as the *Trail-Hunters* of the party. In course, there'll be others adoptin' the same profession, but we'll have to do the big business, and ain't there fun ahead ? Whoop !"

The joyous Dingle gave a leap in the air, and executed a sort of double-shuffle in the bushes for a few moments, when he asked :

"What do you think of it, Peter ?"

"I always wanted to be an Indian-fighter like you, Dingle, but there has always been a drawback—a feller is likely to get killed. If I was sure I wouldn't get hurt, wouldn't I walk into the business ? Where is Jim Peterson ? Is he going ?"

"Freeze me to death, do you s'pose he'd go ? *He's* willing enough, and kind of itches to be off ; but since he's settled down with that Frontier Angel she won't let him think of it. But if these imps keep at their tricks much longer, he and Mansfield have both told me they'll make a free fight of it, *sure.*"

"Wal, I s'pose a man feels diffcrent when he gets a pair of white arms around his neck and a couple of blue eyes looking right through him. 'Pears to me *I* should." And Jenkins assumed a most ludicrous expression of visage, while he wrapped his arms lovingly around his rifle.

"He does—that's a fact," added Dingle.

"How do you know, Dick? I heard Peterson once say you'd been married, and the Shawnees done you an ugly turn. Is it so?"

The hunter made no reply for a moment. The stock of his long rifle rested upon the earth, while his arms were folded over the muzzle, and his eyes had the dreamy, vacant look of profound revery. Presently he drew a deep breath and answered, in a voice softened and modulated by feeling:

"I *have been* married, Jenkins, and I once had a child—a little boy. He was the only one I had. There was Injin blood in his mother's heart, but they didn't spare her for that. When they come on old Wetzel's house, they saved Lew and the other two boys, and wiped out the old folks. It was a long while ago, when Boone and me was young men together. Him and me was off hunting, and it was done while I was gone. They carried 'em both off first, till the little boy told 'em his father's name, when they tomahawked 'em both. Peterson come out in these parts about then, and, as he believed they'd served his gal—that Frontier Angel—the same way, we clapped hands and declared war aginst the whole Injin race. Jim has got his gal back agin, and he has stopped fightin' for awhile. *When I get my boy back I'll stop.* But that can't be, and so I expect to fight till I go under by some of 'em."

"Jenkins," resumed Dingle, after a pause, "*never* agin speak of this as long as I live. If I go under before you, you may tell of it then, but not before." Great, manly tears rolled from his eyes down over his rough cheeks, which he bent over his rifle to hide.

For a few moments not a word was spoken by either. When Dingle looked up his face had lost all traces of emotion, and wore the same stolid expression that characterized it.

"Wal, Jenkins," he said, drawing a deep breath, and throwing his rifle over his shoulder, "it's getting well along, and the clearings are a good tramp from hereabouts. So let's pull up moccasirs."

With this the two trail-hunters turned and disappeared in the forest.

CHAPTER II

THE INTERVIEW IN THE FOREST.

An unusual commotion was felt along the frontier. In nearly all the settlements there were evidences of excitement. Men were seen hurrying to and fro ; scouts were arriving and departing daily ; now and then an Indian runner made his appearance, and, merely halting, hurried away into the forest again. It was plainly evident that some important movement was on foot.

From Western Tennessee the voice of supplication had come. The feeble settlements in that section were exposed to the fury of the savages. Every night the sky was illumined with the flames of cabins, and the agonized shrieks of the white victims pierced the air. First an Indian runner (a faithful Moravian, who had survived the terrible and unholy massacre at Gnadenhutten, by the whites) arrived with a message to William Whitley, imploring him to repair at once to their assistance. This brave man, like a true Kentuckian, without waiting to petition government, instantly pledged himself and called for volunteers.

His own settlement could not be expected to furnish even one-half the required number. He therefore dispatched his scouts to the villages above them on the Ohio, for assistance in the expedition. At the time named the work was only commenced, but it was progressing nobly. The inhabitant of Ohio or Kentucky was never the one to resist the appeal of the weak and suffering.

The settlement to which we ask particular attention for a time, is the seat of Captain Whitley's operations, and which may properly be termed his head-quarters. It was built much after the manner of the Old Fort at Boonesborough : that is, a wall of buildings and palisades inclosed and protected the village. It had two gates, constantly guarded, as also were the forts at the corners. The whole arrangements of forts and houses were a model of a frontier settlement.

Within the inclosure were some thirty or forty cabins, clumsy and unsightly, but precisely what their inhabitants desired. They were built without regard to appearance, and were located according to the taste of their builders. On one side of the village, about a dozen rods distant, flowed the Ohio, while on the opposite stretched the almost interminable forests and cane-brakes of Kentucky. The intervening clear-ing was dotted by black, charred stumps which the fire had failed to destroy.

On the day in question, the gates were thrown open, and the forms of men were constantly passing and repassing through them. Now and then the painted plumes of a savage flitted among the somber-looking whites, and, on several occasions, their long, thrilling signals awoke the forest-echoes. Far down the gleaming Ohio, canoes were moving like tiny birds in the distance. Animation was visible in every coun-tenance, and promptness in every movement. Prominent among the settlers was the gallant Dingle, moving to and fro, and assisting as much by his counsel as by his actions. His tall, muscular form was ever conspicuous.

But, to an ordinary observer, Peter Jenkins would have seemed the most important. He really appeared to be omni-present. Now giving some parting word to one as he rowed away in a canoe ; hurrying across the clearing to communicate with some returning scout ; asking of the most prominent whether "it wasn't best to wear uniform," and also if "it wouldn't be a good plan to kill every Indian in the country." Several times he might be heard giving orders to those around him. The only difficulty in the latter case was that no one gave the least heed to them.

All through the day the din and confusion of preparation went on. Captain Whitley himself had the majority of vol-unteers on a broad space within the clearing, where he was putting them through all sorts of movements, drills and maneuvers, which could possibly come in use in the contem-plated expedition. His eye sparkled with exultation as he saw their enthusiasm and the aptness with which all his orders were executed. There was not a laggard in the whole settlement.

2

As night settled over the wood, all drew within the pallisades, the gates were closed, every thing secured, and the sentinels stationed. There was no expectation of an attack, but the habit of caution had almost become an instinct on the frontier, both among the settlers and Indians. Captain Whitley advised all who were not on guard to retire for the night; but the thoughts of the morrow were too strong and exciting to permit slumber to visit many. The majority, after a time, withdrew to the cabins, while others clustered in groups, and spent the night in speculations upon their future movements.

An hour or so before midnight, the faint call of the whippowil was heard in the forest. Almost immediately the form of a female emerged from a cabin, at one extremity of the village, and made her way toward the western gate. She stole her way carefully along, as if fearing observation. When at the gate, she shrunk silently within its shadow, where she remained a few moments, as though irresolute and undecided. In a moment, she uttered a suppressed call to the sentinel.

"Hello, Miss Maude, is that you?" was the call in return.

"Yes; hurry and let me through."

"I don't know, Maude, whether I should. I shouldn't wonder if there's somebody in them woods besides Monowano. I heard his call just now, but, confound them Shawnees, there's no trusting them."

"Let me out, Tom; there's no danger, I assure you."

"The fact is, you know, I've got orders not to open this gate after nightfall for white or red. Howsumever, I believe it's generally understood that we are to let you go. So hurry along with you, and don't remain in the woods too long, or you may be shut out for the night."

With this, the sentinel carefully withdrew the bolt, and Maude glided quickly out. She sped across the clearing, and, in a moment, disappeared in the wood. Within this, she hurried some twenty or thirty rods, and then paused beside a large fallen tree. A moment after, a light step was heard, and a lithe, graceful form, clad in the habiliments of an Indian warrior, glided beside her.

"I heard your call, Monowano," she said, as the Indian took

her hand, "but I was delayed so long at the gate that I feared you had gone."

"Monowano never fled from the light of the Evening Star," replied the warrior, using the figurative language of his race, and giving to Maude the name by which he always addressed her. "When the light of morning comes, and the star of the evening departs, then Monowano seeks the home of his people."

"Have you seen the preparations to march against you?"

"Monowano has hid in the woods, and from his seat in the tree-tops counted their number. They are many, and when the other Long Knives unite, they will drive back the Shaw-nee warriors from the Ohio."

"And what will you do in this struggle?"

"These hands of mine," said the warrior, pressing those of Maude, "have never shed the blood of a pale-face, and shall never be raised against him."

"Will you fight with our people?"

The savage started, as if stung, and quickly replied:

"And never shall Monowano fight against the Shawnees. He shall befriend both people. When the red-men gather like the autumn-leaves in the forest-hollows, he shall warn the pale-faces; and when the Shawnee sleeps, and dreams of his squaw and children, and the Long Knife steals like the serpent upon him, Monowano shall shout and save his kindred."

"Be careful," said Maude, lowering her voice; "the whites are angry, and they will kill you if they suspect you help your people."

"Monowano is known to his white brothers, and can he not die for his people?" asked the savage, haughtily. "If the pale-faces seek to slay him, he cares not."

"They will not," said Maude, affectionately, "unless you provoke them. Don't do it, Monowano, for my sake. Will you remain here when they go forth?"

"When the Long Knives take the war-path, Monowano will follow them, as the dog follows the deer. He will never slumber."

"I do not fear—"

"Hist!" interrupted the Indian, turning his head; "some one watches."

Both listened, but Maude heard nothing, save the beating

of her own heart, and the faint sighing of the wind overhead. Her attendant had drawn his knife, and stood in that crouching, panther-like attitude of intense attention, in which one of those curious similarities between the animal and Indian is so plainly brought out. The light of the moon, piercing the tree-tops, shone full upon his face, revealing one of singular beauty. His brows were contracted, and his head bent, so that the ornamented scalp-lock suffered the eagle-feathers to dangle before his waist. One arm was rigid, and closed tightly over his knife, while the other rested upon the handle of his tomahawk at his waist. Neither stirred for a few moments, when Maude asked:

"Do you hear any thing more?"

"He has fled. Some one has heard our words, and will spread them to the winds. It is well that he is not here now."

The Indian replaced his knife as he spoke, and turned toward Maude. The latter, looking up in his face, asked:

"When shall I see you again?"

Her companion pointed at the moon, now in its crescent.

"When she is full and round, and lights up the war-path which the Long Knives have taken, and the Shawnees have fled before them, then Monowano will return. When the shadows fall upon the forest, and the whippowil calls, let the Evening Star shed its light for Monowano."

"She will ever listen for the song of the whippowil, for it is the sweetest song of all the birds of the wood."

"And the light of the Evening Star is the life of Monowano," added the Indian, his eyes flashing with the warmth of his words.

For a half-hour longer the two conversed, each heart glowing with love and affection for the other, and yet no demonstration, more than the mere pressing of the hands of Maude by her Indian lover, was offered. Finally, they separated as silently as they had come together; the warrior disappeared like a shadow in the wood, and the maiden sped noiselessly across the clearing to the gate, where the sentinel admitted her, and she hurried to her own cabin.

Monowano was the name of one who was well known to the settlement referred to in this chapter. He was supposed to be the son of a chieftain of the Shawnees; but his singular beauty led many to the supposition that he was part white. Others affirmed he was a younger brother of Tecumseh, who was coming into notice at this time. He was of the same stature and form as that renowned chief, and was as graceful and athletic in his movements. He was always clothed in the gaudy dress of the sachems, with a head-dress of eagle feathers dyed in many brilliant colors. The majority believed him to be a devoted friend to the whites, but there were not wanting a number who secretly envied the savage his popularity, and did their utmost against him. They reported him a spy, and assured their credulous friends that the time would come when his treachery would evince itself. This feeling of distrust and suspicion had gained considerable ground during the last few weeks. The unusual absence of the Indian, together with the petition from the settlers in West Tennessee for succor, confirmed many in the belief that he was in league with the hostile Shawnees. In short, Monowano had been made aware that he would be running a great risk by showing himself to the settlers in their present state of feeling.

About a year before, while in the settlement, this Indian participated in a drill of the militia, and discovered a wonderful amount of military knowledge, imparting to the whites many useful hints in regard to the execution of different maneuvers and stratagems. This rendered him a person of importance in the eyes of the settlers, and, at the same time, an object of suspicion to the few referred to. It was on this occasion that he became acquainted with Maude Burland, an orphan, and the ward of a Mr. Mordaunt, one of the most influential settlers. The handsome, manly form of the Indian made its impression upon the heart of Maude; and, at the same time, he did not strive to conceal his admiration for the modest, dark-eyed maiden. Mordaunt detected the attachment at once, and endeavored to prevent its consummation; but he soon saw that this was impossible, and, like a sensible man, said no more about it.

For a while Monowano visited Maude at her home in the settlement; but he never felt easy under the suspicious glances of those around him, and ever since the snow had melted from the forest, the two had met within it. Twice every week the Indian's signal was heard by the sentinels, and

Maude was allowed to pass out of the gates to him. In spite of the suspicion attending his movements, he had not failed to enter occasionally the village, until the last few weeks, during which time none but Maude had seen him.

CHAPTER III.

INCIDENTS BY THE WAY.

"The morn brought the marshaling in arms," and the day, "battle's magnificently stern array." Ere the sun was fairly above the wilderness, the whole settlement was in commotion. A runner had arrived during the night with the intelligence that the depredations of the Shawnees were continued, and the people, such as were able, were arming themselves. Colonel Orr had promised to meet Captain Whitley, at a rendezvous which the latter had appointed, with five hundred volunteers, and the utmost dispatch was required.

Orders were issued by the captain for preparations to be made for marching at once. All forces expected from neighboring settlements were on the ground, when it was found they numbered about a hundred men. These were summoned on the clearing in front of the settlement, where Captain Whitley briefly addressed them. It needed no eloquence of his to inspire them with ardor. He read their determination in flashing eyes and heaving breasts. Each man clutched his rifle, and seemed impatient for the coming contest. At nine o'clock the order of march was taken up. Amid the tears and farewells, the cheers and good wishes of those left behind, the gallant little band wound across the clearing, like some huge serpent gliding into the mighty forest.

This expedition against the Nickajack towns is the first one in American history which has the credit of using *mounted artillery*. Whitley (who was now constituted colonel by his own troops) mounted a swivel *upon his horse*, so arranged that he could wheel and fire in any direction. He was also provided with nearly fifty balls of wrought iron, and, perhaps, might have been properly termed a fort in himself. As he remarked, in case of pursuit he would be able to halt and stand quite a siege.

As soon as the forest was fairly entered, the scouts scattered, and betook themselves to their several duties. They were instructed to outlie the troops, constantly communicate with each other, and, in no cases, except as a signal of danger, were any, save the two hunters in the rear, to discharge their rifles. Dingle and Jenkins were denominated the *trail-hunters* of the party, and were to scour the forest in front, to guard against any ambush of their enemy, and to detect and report every sign of their presence.

A fatal policy seems to have attended, for a time, every movement of the Americans against their Indian enemies. The disastrous defeats of Bowman, Clark, Harmar, and St. Clair followed each other in succession, and will ever be a blot upon our military achievements on the frontier. In all of these campaigns the causes will be found to be the same— the incompetency of their leaders. That they were brave men can not be denied ; but they lacked that perfect command and control over their troops, without which no general can successfully meet an enemy in any way equal. That perfect discipline can not always repel an Indian assault, is proved by the sad fate of the British general, Braddock, and his force ; but it was their admirable discipline that in the end prevented their total extermination. Had this brilliant commander possessed one tithe of the knowledge of Indian tactics that our own generals had, it can not be doubted that his courage would have prevailed. The troops, by not hesitating to put themselves under the directions of young Washington, at the fall of their leader, saved themselves, as said, from annihilation.

Captain Whitley was a man to whom these defeats taught their lesson, and he has properly received credit for the masterly manner in which he conducted the "Nickajack Expedition."

The one hundred volunteers marched rapidly to the rendezvous, where, as expected, they found Colonel Orr awaiting them with five hundred men. Whitley and Orr, both colonels, concluded to cast lots for the command. This was done, and it was found that Whitley was chosen.

The six hundred fell into order at once, and, turning their faces toward Tennessee, plunged into the forest. Nearly twenty miles of the intended route lay through a range of mountains, which it was determined were to be crossed at night. On either side of this force were some half-dozen scouts flitting silently through the wood. Sometimes their forms could be discerned coiled up in the limbs of a tree, and the next instant they would rise from behind some log, or whisk through the bushes like startled animals. Now and then the shots in the rear showed that the hunters were not unmindful of their duty.

On the western side of the force were three men who were numbered among the most skillful scouts and Indian-fighters on the frontier. These three, about noon, might have been seen together, their heads bent, and conversing in low tones. One had stooped, and was carefully raking the leaves with the stock of his rifle.

"What do you make of it, Jim?" asked one of his companions.

"A moccasin."

"Delaware, Wyandot, or Shawnee?"

"Ugh! who are we huntin' for? If a Shawnee hasn't broke that stick less than an hour ago, then a red has never yelped in old Kaintuck."

"Only one?"

"Only one; some infarnal spy, somewhere 'round us now. 'Twon't do for him to get into Nickajack with the news. We must get his top-knot."

"How is it Dingle hasn't seen the trail?"

"'Spect he has, but didn't think it worth while to tell us 'bout it. 'Tain't in his line to see it."

The three scouts now knelt, and on their knees examined the trail. Suddenly one gave a suppressed laugh:

"Call that Shawnee, do you? Toes turned out! Ha! ha!"

"Freeze me if it ain't so, Jim," added the other. "What's the matter with your peepers?"

"Nothing," returned the one addressed as Jim. "Toes twisted inward or outward, *it's a Shawnee.*"

The others gazed at him as if they suspected his sanity.

"You needn't stare at me so," he retorted. "Have either of you ever heard of a Shawnee called Monowano?"

An expression of intelligence flashed over the faces of the two addressed. All three knew Monowano well, and were aware of a curious fact in regard to him. The Indian had a habit of slightly inclining his feet outward when walking, a peculiarity which no other savage had evinced, and which had often been remarked by the settlers. One of these same scouts was the most inveterate enemy of the Shawnee.

"What business has he sneaking 'round us this way?"

"Looks suspicious, that's a fact."

"I've always said that fellow had mischief in him, though it seemed hard to make the others believe it. Injin is Injin wherever you find him; and if Colonel Whitley was of my mind, that Monowano wouldn't trouble him much longer."

"It may be that Dingle hasn't seen this trail, so I'll give him the hint."

With this, Jim Botts shot silently off to the left, and a few minutes after made his appearance beside Dick Dingle, who was just then conversing with Jenkins. As he heard Botts' footsteps he turned toward him, inquiring, by the expression of his countenance, what his errand was.

"Sign?" interrogated the latter.

"Yes; what of it."

"You know him?"

"Monowano."

"All right; remember, Whitley has given orders to bring in every spy we can lay hands on."

"Monowano ain't a spy," replied Dingle, quietly.

"P'raps so," added Botts, with a meaning shake of his head.

"Do you know he is?" asked Dingle, fixing his keen eyes upon the speaker.

"All I've got to say is that if I cotched a man trying to break into my house, I'd venture to set him down as a robber; and if I cotches a redskin skulking through the woods, keeping watch upon a lot of soldiers, I'd undertake to suspect him to be a spy."

"Wal, Jim Botts, you can allow them pegs of your'n to carry you away from here about as quick as you please. You're a good hunter, but you know you've no business to think Monowano wants to harm us. I don't stick up fur njins generally, but I does for that chap. Howsumever, when we encamp I'll bring him before Whitley, and you may question him as much as you please. You needn't take the pains to come to me agin with any of your idees."

"There's no need of getting mad about it," replied Botts, with a rueful countenance, as he moved away. So soon as he was out of hearing, Dingle turned toward Jenkins.

"This looks bad for Monowano, Pete. I'd swear my life if that paint was rubbed off his face you'd find white skin under it; and as for him bein' a spy, the thing is onpossible. He's hangin' round fur sunkthin; and if the boys see him, he'll be shot if they can't capture him; so he'll have to be brought in if we can find him."

"I don't see how you're going to lay hand on the mink, for he takes to the woods like a duck to water, and I even doubt *my* ability to entrap him, so cunning and careful is he."

"He isn't fur off, and if he thinks *we* want him, the fellow will come in, for he prides himself a heap upon his honor. Let's move on, and keep your peepers peeled fur sign."

With this, the two moved forward in their usual cautious manner. It was not until the middle of the afternoon, however, that they again found visible signs of Monowano's presence. Jenkins' attention was attracted to Dingle by a low, peculiar whistle of the latter.

"What's up now?"

"Look!" he replied, pointing downward upon a piece of moss. Jenkins did as directed, and saw the two well known prints of the Indian's moccasins.

"He's done it on purpose; he's within call."

Dingle gave a sharp, suppressed whistle, as a signal which was well known to the savage. This was repeated several times, but no answer was received.

"Perhaps he's forgotten how to whistle," said Jenkins. "Wait till he has practiced a little, and you'll hear him."

"Monowano has no fear of the white man," repeated that individual himself, stepping from behind a tree, and approaching the two whites.

"Hello! that you? how are you?" ejaculated Jenkins, with a visible start, and partly retreating behind Dingle.

"Monowano, you must go with me," said the latter, stepping forward to meet him.

"Where?" asked the savage, with a slight recoil.

"To the encampment; the men have found out that you're hangin' round, and it'll be the safest plan."

The Indian folded his arms, signifying his willingness to comply with the hunter's wish.

"You don't think, Monowano, I'd play you false?" asked Dingle, in a tone of uncertainty.

"Monowano has no fear of his White Father," replied the Indian, quietly.

"All right; I'll answer for your safety. I don't think Captain Whitley would dare to hurt you if he knew I was set agin it. I don't think he would dare," repeated Dingle, as if talking to himself. "He has known me long enough to know my temper, and if Captain Whitley or any of his men should shoot this Injin, *I'd shoot him!*"

"How is it there's such a friendship between you and him? and what makes him call you his 'White Father?'" asked Jenkins.

"It's what he has always called me—jist a notion of his I s'pose. If I thought Monowano, standing there, was a spy, I'd save the captain the trouble of shooting him; but I've know'd him long enough to know we haven't got a better friend than him; and though I hate all his people like rank pizen, I'm bound to see that *he's* used right. Yes, sir."

The trail-hunter compressed his lips and shook his head determinedly, as he uttered these words.

"Just so," added Jenkius. "I see the light is fading around us, and the men have probably camped."

"We'll go in then."

As Dingle moved away, he glanced at the Indian, who had remained as indifferent as a statue during the conversation with Jenkins. The savage followed him with a deliberate pace, and a few minutes later the three made their appearance at the spot where the army had encamped. There was some commotion as the Indian strode proudly forward, with a step as haughty and dignified as the greatest chieftain of his people. He walked directly in front of Dingle, where he halted and gazed around upon the encampment. His dark eyes shone proudly as their eagle-gaze encountered the different officers, as though he were the leader and master of all he saw.

"Ah! who have you there, Dingle?" asked Captain Whitley, coming forward. "Our old friend Monowano, eh? It's a long time since I have met you, Monowano; and yet I must confess I am rather sorry to meet you under these circumstances. Nevertheless, I greet you."

Whitley extended his hand as he spoke; but the Indian remained with folded arms, and, with a look that would have stung a king, deliberately turned his back upon him.

"What are you sorry to meet him fur, captain?" asked Dingle.

"Because it looks bad for him, Dick; I have been told several times during the day, that he was skulking through the wood and watching our movements. Such a thing as that you know would be your or my death-warrant if caught. I have good reason to believe that *Monowano is a spy!*"

"Whoever told you that, Captain Whitley, lies. You haven't a truer man in your company than that Injin, and I'll see justice done him."

"How is it, friend Dingle, that *you* are the one who has brought him in?"

"I know'd he was in the wood, I know'd what this talk was about him, and brought him in that he might have a fair trial."

"And that you may rest assured he shall have. You two men there, bring the Indian to my camp, and see that he is well watched."

"All right, but don't you undertake to bind him," said Dingle to the two men. "There's no danger of his tryin' to run away. Ef there was, he wouldn't have come in so easy."

The Indian followed the two men, who appeared as though they were menials clearing the way for an emperor. He was ushered into a tent, where were seated Captain Whitley and a number of officers. A seat was offered Monowano, but he declined it, and remained standing, his arms folded in the usual manner, and his face perfectly calm and stoical.

"Monowano," said Captain Whitley, respectfully, "I would fain believe you to be a true friend to us. But your actions for the past few months have given us good reason to doubt you. Why do you watch us thus? What reason have you for thus dodging through the wood?"

"Why does the eagle sail above the clouds? Why does the deer live in the woods? Has Manitou told them that the pale-face forbids it?" asked the Indian, bending his dark eyes upon those of his interlocutor.

"All true—all true," replied Whitley. "We don't pretend or wish to prevent the deer or Indian from roaming over his own hunting-ground. We don't object to that at all; but the deer flees from the white man; he does not follow him."

"The eagle watches the antelope from the clouds, and follows him whither he wills."

"Very true, Monowano, but the eagle does that, you know, to fall upon and slay the antelope at last. And it is the same object, we fear, that leads you to follow and watch us as you have."

As this direct charge was uttered against the Indian, his head turned as quick as lightning upon Whitley. The latter expecting a reply, braved his glance. But the Indian said nothing. After waiting a few moments, the captain repeated his charge, and asked several questions. But it was all in vain. The lips of the Indian were sealed, and no mortal threats or power could open them. Whitley and his officers consulted together, and the Indian was led away, when Dick Dingle, the trail-hunter, made his appearance. He was questioned closely, and gave every particular of the capture—if such it could be termed—of the Indian. He was then allowed to remain and help determine what should be done. He found that Whitley and every one was in favor of having him shot at once. To this Dingle demurred, and becoming somewhat excited, wound up by swearing that he would shoot the man or every one who assisted in his execution; after which he declared he would turn renegade, and spend the rest of his life in warring against the whites.

After this forcible expression, Whitley informed Dingle that he might retire, and the fate of Monowano would be determined without further aid from him.

"It is strange," said the captain, after the trail-hunter had departed. "I am unwilling as any one to believe that our prisoner is guilty; yet, positively, I can see no other view which can be taken of this affair. Monowano's conduct is inexplicable; indeed, he makes no attempt to explain it. If he be a spy he ought to die, and *shall die*, too, if there is any power in what I say. I do not like this threat of Dingle's, as I know he would carry it out, and he is too valuable a man to lose; yet, it should not deter me in my duty. Dingle would not be so positive in the innocence of the Indian had he not good reason for it. Were it any other man, I should be tempted to doubt his honesty; but there is no treachery in *him*."

"Could we not compromise the matter by retaining Mono wano as a prisoner, until our expedition has terminated?" asked one of the officers.

Captain Whitley shook his head.

"He would escape, and would then most certainly be our inveterate enemy. No; I must admit that I am in a dilemma, caused by the lingering doubt of the Indian's guilt."

A long consultation was held, the result of which was the acquittal of Monowano. Captain Whitley could not rid himself of the partial belief in his innocence, and he was too conscientious a man to punish him under such circumstances. Several of the officers finally agreed that this course seemed best. The soldiers themselves were considerably surprised, for they counted upon the Indian's death as certain.

Captain Whitley, in a private conversation with Dingle, informed him of his decision, adding that it resulted entirely from the doubt of which we have spoken, and from no threats of his. He further informed the hunter that he might take Monowano to a distance from the camp; and, after giving him some good advice, allowed him to depart.

At a late hour, Dingle, accompanied by the Indian, struck off into the wood. Not a syllable was spoken by either until they reached the bank of a large creek. Here Dingle halted, and, turning toward his companion, said:

"We must part on this spot, Monowano. I don't know what your notion is in hangin' round us so, and I'd advise you to try some other means of amusin' yourself. But, good luck to you."

The Indian stepped in front of Dingle, and raising his arm, pointed to the moon.

"Before that is round and full, Monowano will show his White Father that he remembers him; Monowano will never forget."

With this brief but expressive remark, the Indian strode down the bank of the stream, and, turning off to the left, was lost to view in the wood. Dingle remained motionless a moment, as if in deep thought, and then made his way to the encampment.

CHAPTER IV

THE MOST REMARKABLE TRAIL-HUNT ON RECORD.

IT was the determination of Whitley that the distance of fifteen miles which led over the mountains should be crossed during the night. This was necessary in order to make the surprise of the Nickajack towns complete. They lay upon the opposite side, and unless Monowano should prove treacherous, could as yet have no knowledge of the expedition against them.

The mountains were reached in the early part of the afternoon, when a halt was made to continue until nightfall. The usual sentinel and guards were stationed, when Dingle and Jenkins set out in the woods to ascertain whether any suspicious trails were to be seen in the vicinity. A mile from the camp, Jenkins said:

"I propose, Dingle, that we part and hunt for sign separately. I flatter myself that I won't cross any thing suspicious without observing it, and the chances, you see, are thus doubled for each of us."

"All right," responded Dingle. "You see the captain is very wishful that the Injins shouldn't find out that we're about, and so, I take it, it would be best to spend your time all night in searching the wood."

"My sentiments exactly."

And the two separated. Dingle, we may remark, after several hours' careful search, discovered nothing upon which he could hang a suspicion, and reported the fact to Whitley upon his return in the evening. Jenkins had a different experience, however.

After parting from Dingle, he spent an hour in wandering aimlessly forward, not heeding or caring where his steps led him, as he well knew he could find his way back to camp again.   Suddenly he discovered the print of a footstep upon the leaves before him.

"Hello!" he exclaimed with a start, "there's sign as sure as the world.   Some infarnal Injin is scouting through the woods.   Wonder whether it's Monowano?   No; the print is too big for him.   Some chief, I'll warrant.   There's a mighty responsibility resting upon me.   Perhaps the success of the Nickajack expedition depends entirely upon my exertions.   I must follow up the trail, and either kill or capture the audacious spy."

Ducking his head downward, like a crouching animal, and trailing his rifle, he started upon a half-trot, and a half-walk. He had a keen eye, and followed the trail readily.   He was very careful not to disturb it, but to keep to one side.   The last wish of Jenkins was to encounter the Indian who, he believed, was thus leading him on.   His long companionship with Dingle had given him much skill in tracking a foe; and he felt confident that his ignorance would not bring him into a collision.   From the evidence of the different signs, he was satisfied that he was an hour or so only in the rear.

"Whoever he is, he certainly has no suspicion that Peter Jenkins is upon his trail.   He appears as though he invited his own destruction.   The tracks are hardly large enough to be those of the chief Big Foot, and they slightly incline outward.   Ah!   I understand it it's an artifice to deceive us. But Peter Jenkins is too shrewd a person to have the wool pulled over his eyes in that manner.   Yes, sir, as Dingle says."

The pursuit was maintained with the persistency of the blood-hound, and soon resulted in another most important discovery.   Jenkins came upon a spot where the Indian had encountered another of his tribe.   They appeared to have consulted together a few moments and then to have separated and taken different directions.   Jenkins halted but a moment, and then resumed his duty, determined to keep the original trail.

Nearly an hour afterward, and to his unbounded amazement, he discovered that he was not following one Indian but *two!* The tracks were too plain to be mistaken, and he stopped a few minutes to think the matter over.

"Things begin to look dangerous," he muttered. "Here are two prowling savages within a few miles of the camp. They must be reconnoitering in the woods this very minute. I must learn more of this, although it's a terrible risk I run in chasing up two infuriated denizens of the wilderness. Dingle and the boys, from their actions, seem to think *I'm afraid* to do what they have sometimes done, and I'll show them I ain't. I might signal for Dingle to come and help me, but then, like as not, he'd have something to say about my being scar't. So, I'll go it alone for a time yet at any rate."

He moved with the greatest caution, as he felt he was gradually gaining upon his enemies. If he should unexpectedly stumble upon them, the consequences, to say the least, would be unpleasant. Moving thus forward, and occasionally communing with himself, he was brought to a stand-still once more, with a

"Whew! by thunder!"

The fact was, the leaves before him showed unmistakably the footprints of *three savages!*

"Matters are getting more serious every minute. There is some deep plot on foot. It may be that a large Indian force is outlying in the woods and meditate an attack this evening. I should like to discover their whereabouts and intentions myself; but it is too prodigious an undertaking, and I must have the co-operation of Dingle."

Placing his fingers in his mouth, he gave a sharp, peculiar whistle, repeating it three times. A moment after, an answer came from toward the mountains, and, leaning against a tree, he awaited the appearance of Dingle.

"What's up?" asked the latter in a whisper, as he emerged to view. Jenkins answered by pointing to the trail before him. The hunter examined it a moment, and then merely said:

"Lead the way and I'll foller."

The two glided forward as noiselessly as serpents. The ground disappeared rapidly beneath them, and Jenkins' heart

3

beat high as he reflected that he was leading the most distinguished scout in their force upon a duty that would reflect the highest credit upon him when its result came to be reported to the captain.

It was nearly sunset, when Jenkins' hair fairly lifted the hat from his head as he saw the footprints before him all at once increase to five. As Dingle said nothing, however, he kept on, determined to maintain the hunt as long as his companion dared follow.

How much longer this remarkable trail-hunt might have continued, it is impossible to tell. Jenkins was electrified by hearing a suppressed chuckling noise behind him. Turning, instantly, he saw Dingle leaning against a tree, seemingly ready to drop to the earth with the excess of his mirth. A light flashed upon his brain, and he gasped:

"My Heavens! Dingle, don't tell any one of this!"

"*Follerin' your own trail!*" exclaimed the hunter, suppressing his mirth for the instant.

CHAPTER V

THE ATTACK AND THE RESULT.

As the shades of night settled over the forest, preparations were made for commencing the march through the mountains. Before it was fairly dark, the men were under way and the first range was reached. Here a formidable difficulty was experienced. The thick forest made the darkness intense; and, as but one or two knew the direction to the Indian towns, there was great danger of the different companies becoming separated and bewildered. The success of the expedition depended upon a quick and well ordered march. A war-path led in a direct line to the Indian towns, and it was imperatively necessary that this path should not be lost by one of the men.

A few minutes' reflection gave Captain Whitley the means of relief. A number of knots of resinous pine were fired and carried at the head of each party, and the march was renewed with certainty and vigor.

They formed a singular and ghostly company, these volunteers. A long train of shadowy forms, gliding like specters over the narrow war-path, the flaring torches serving to light up a few of the bronzed faces, and the only sound heard, the dull, regular tramp of the numerous feet. Several hundred yards in advance, some six or eight scouts, led by Dick Dingle, and driven by Peter Jenkins, could now and then be discerned as they crossed the different openings in the wood. In the pale moonlight, they looked like a company of chained culprits, marching to the scaffold. Their heads were bent, and their ears constantly on the alert for the least suspicious sound.

Sometimes they made their appearance upon the banks of a creek or smaller stream, and halted a few moments until the main body came up. They then stepped noiselessly into the water, and ascended the opposite bank like so many beavers, and wound into the wood again.

Mile after mile was passed through the gloomy arches of the forest, through the tangled undergrowth, up the rugged defiles of the mountains, down the precipitous sides, over streams and gullies, and, by midnight, they were within five miles of the Nickajack towns.

They were ascending the last range, when Jenkins jumped out of the path, and, running forward to Dingle, whispered:

" There's an Injin or an animal following us! I've heard him along side of me two—three times."

" I know it," replied Dingle; " I heard him, and am on the look-out for him. Jest keep your place, Pete, and be careful he don't nab you. If you see him, rush in and grab him, and if you hold him till I come up I'll promise never to let out a word about that *trail-hunt*. Ogh!"

" I'll be darned if I don't do it."

Jenkins slipped back to his place in the rear. He asked the man in front of him to carry his rifle a short time, under some pretense, in order that he might have his arms free for the desperate duty he had resolved upon. As may be supposed, it required a great deal of mental torment for Jenkins to bring himself to this point. But he succeeded at last.

Ever since his unfortunate adventure at the block-house with the Frontier Angel, he had been anxious to accomplish some deed that would free Dingle of the doubt and suspicion he entertained of his courage. Of course this could not be done unless he really underwent some danger, for his companion was too shrewd a man to be deceived by any artifice he could invent. The present, therefore, was a good occasion for him to retrieve his good name, not only with Dingle, but with the rest of his acquaintances.

In a few minutes he heard the stealthy footstep again. Fearful that the others might also detect it, and prevent him carrying out his determination, he resolved to lose no time. He strained his eyes to pierce the intense gloom, and finally believed he could now and then detect a shadowy form flitting beside him. Drawing a deep breath, he made a bound toward it, and, spreading out his arms, closed them around the form of an Indian !

"I've got him ! quick ! help ! or he'll get away !"

Before the men, near as they were, could reach him, Jenkins felt a pair of vice-like arms close around him and lift him bodily from the ground. The next instant he went spinning through the air like a frog, and fell directly upon the head of Dingle, who had not left the war-path.

"Who is this—white or red ?" demanded the indignant hunter, seizing him with his right hand and fairly twisting him to the earth.

"Me ! me ! Pete Jenkins ! Oh Lord ! you'll kill me !"

Dingle relinquished his grasp, and darted away in the wood. As quick as lightning the identity of Jenkins' enemy flashed upon him. He had gone but a rod or so, when a noise like the hiss of a serpent attracted his attention.

"*Monowano !*" he called, in a husky whisper.

"My White Father," was replied at his elbow.

"Keep further away ! keep further away, Monowano ! Ef you're cotched agin I can't do nothin' fur you. Keep off—remember."

"Monowano will heed the words of his White Father."

A minute after, Dingle was leading the scouts onward, as though nothing had occurred to alarm them.

With the exception of Dingle and Jenkins, no one had the

least suspicion that it was the Indian Monowano that had caused such a commotion for an instant among them. Jenkins affirmed positively that it was some ferocious wild animal—most propably a panther—that had used him so roughly, and Dingle, for evident reasons, sustained him in his assertions.

An hour or two before daybreak, the scouts halted at the base of the last range of mountains, and waited for the soldiers to come up. Shortly after, Captain Whitley and his officers made their appearance, and the whole force formed in order for battle. Dingle and three others were sent forward to reconnoiter the village, while Whitley and Orr consulted together. In a half-hour Dingle returned with the intelligence that the entire town was wrapped in slumber, and unsuspicious of any danger.

This was the town which Captain Whitley was the most anxious to attack. Its members had committed more ravages in Tennessee than any other tribe. Scores of white scalps hung in their lodges, and their tomahawks were ever red with the blood of innocent victims. In the present weakened state of the government, the power of these savages was too great to be broken. Captain Whitley therefore determined to do his utmost to accomplish this by one stroke.

Orders were given to surround the town as quietly as possible. As all of the volunteers were skilled in Indian warfare, this was accomplished successfully. Dingle and Jenkins, as usual, were in company.

It was now nearly daybreak. The soldiers were hardly placed in position, when an Indian dog barked, and three savages were seen moving through the village. Several guns were discharged, as a signal for attack, and the battle commenced at once.

A murderous volley was poured into the wigwams, and a simultaneous rush made upon them. The Indians, roused from slumber, fought with the fury of desperation. The tomahawk met the thrust of the knife, and the flash of the Indian rifle that of the American. Wild, chilling whoops rent the air, and the stern order of the chiefs could be heard amid the shouts of the excited volunteers. A company of determined Indians made a break in the lines, and through this their squaws, children and themselves rushed pell-mell like so many affrighted sheep.

Dick Dingle was among the first who dashed forward, and his exertions proved him a host within himself. Right and left the Indians fell around him, and, leaping over their fallen bodies, he burst into a wigwam. At this instant some one applied a torch, and in an incredible space of time the village was one sheet of flame. The combustible material of the different lodges flashed up like powder, and made the scene of the conflict as bright as noonday. As Dingle broke into the lodge, his head encountered something, and he fell, partly stunned, to the earth. Ere he could rise, half a dozen Indians pounced upon him, and he felt the iron twist of his matted hair preparatory to its being "raised."

"You've got Dick Dingle at last," said the hunter, as he ceased his efforts. "Hurry up and yank off his top-knot, and wipe him out as quick as you can make it convenient."

A hand wrenched his hair several times, and then his enemies seemed to dispute about something. Dingle resolutely kept his face to the ground, determined not to look up as long as he could help. But, instead of being scalped and brained, he felt the great load upon him all at once removed, and himself dragged rapidly through the blazing lodge, out into the open air, where some one whispered excitedly in his ear :

"Run ! run ! be careful !"

Springing to his feet, he darted away into the thickest of the combat ; but not until he had given a look of thankfulness to his preserver—Monowano.

The battle ceased almost instantly. The town was in ruins, fifty Indians were slain, nineteen taken prisoners, and the rest had fled.

It was now daylight, and Captain Whitley, taking with him twenty men, (including Dingle and Jenkins,) commenced a rapid march toward the Running Water town, intending to attack that also. But the alarm had reached it, and they were boldly met by a body of Indians, who charged upon them at the tap of the drum. A regular running bush-fight now occurred. The parties were nearly equal in number and strength, and the warriors fought with the most determined courage. Several times they were compelled to give ground, but their unerring rifles made the soldiers retreat in turn; and the contest was extremely doubtful, until Dingle, heading a charge, routed them completely, killing several of the most prominent warriors. The others fled and escaped.

Whitley, having fully accomplished the object of the expedition, collected his men and set out on his return. He had punished the Indians, and checked the daring outrages which they had so long committed. Several of his own men had been killed, and, before they had reached home, it was discovered that Jenkins was missing. From inquiries made by Dingle, it was rendered certain that in the charge which he headed, Jenkins had been captured and carried off by the retreating Indians. One of the men had seen him seized, and another affirmed that he saw him, in company with several warriors, tearing through the wood, as if in mortal fear of his own kindred.

CHAPTER VI.

SHOWING THAT THE RACE IS NOT ALWAYS TO THE SWIFT.

How Peter Jenkins was captured by the Indians no one ever learned. Even that individual himself professed to be completely in the dark when he endeavored to account for it. The most probable explanation is the one given by himself. During the charge of Dingle, he unexpectedly found himself face to face with three swarthy Indians. Just as he was on the point of assaulting the whole three, he was most unaccountably taken with one of his *fainting-fits*. When consciousness dawned upon him, he found he was running over the ground at a terrific rate, there being a savage on either side of him, with a firm hold upon his collar.

He remonstrated against this, affirming that the Indians "tickled" him so much that he could scarcely breathe. He was, however, hurried forward with unabated speed, and in a short time arrived at Running Water town completely exhausted and out of breath. When his captors loosened their hold, he dropped like a rag to the ground; but two or three well applied kicks brought him to his feet again.

It is not to be supposed that Jenkins was insensible of the great peril in which he was placed. Captured as he was, as an enemy, directly after the fearful defeat of the Indians, there could be no grounds for hoping for liberty or ransom. He was too well secured to think of freeing himself, and in the broad daylight it was utterly out of the question. Jenkins could only see one loop-hole of escape—if it even could be termed that—and that was Monowano.

He knew the Indian was the soul of honor, and, when his unfortunate situation was discovered, would do all he could for him. But there were times when the highest chief of the tribe could not stay the fury of the warriors, and such a time he had every reason to believe was the present. Still, a man having the mortal fear of death that Jenkins had was not to be discouraged so long as the slightest hope remained.

He was tied over and over again, and secured in one of the lodges near the center of the village, and guarded by several warriors. He believed the chiefs were debating his fate, and it would shortly be announced to him. So he determined to send for Monowano, while the opportunity remained.

"Any of you chaps know a feller named Monowano?"

The Indians standing around simply gave the prisoner a wondering stare, as though they did not understand his question.

"Monowano I said—any of you know him?"

The Indians now looked at each other and mumbled something in their own tongue, in which Jenkins heard the name of Monowano mentioned once or twice. They then looked at him, as if to invite a repetition of the question.

"Monowano is the chap I mean. I want to see him," said Jenkins, elevating his voice to a high key, as though it would translate his words for them.

The savages gave utterance again to their guttural words, and then turned their faces toward Jenkins, maintaining a strict silence and stoical indifference. He repeated his question several times, but received no reply, and was about really to despair, when Monowano himself entered the lodge. He started as his eyes rested upon his white friend. An expression of pain flitted for an instant over his face, leaving it as cold and unimpassioned as before.

" How do you do, Monowano ?" asked Jenkins, with as much cheerfulness as he could assume.

The Indian took the proffered hand, and then dropping it, and shaking his head, he said, as he retreated a step and assumed the upright position :

" Sorry to see you here—sorry, Jenkins."

" I'm glad to hear it. I'm tremendous sorry myself, and I trust I can soon change my situation through your exertions."

" I'm afraid I can do nothing," replied Monowano, compressing his lips, and averting his face.

Jenkins fairly gasped for breath as the Indian uttered these words, and an overwhelming sense of his danger deprived him almost of consciousness.

" But you can try, Monowano. Did not Dingle and I stand by you when *you* were in danger ? You would have never been here, had it not been for what Dingle and I did for you."

" I know — all true," replied the Indian, much moved. " Monowano will *try ;* but the war-spirit moves mightily in the hearts of his people, and his arm can not stay their will."

" Do you know what they intend doing with me ?" asked Jenkins, in a pleading, wailing tone.

" Can you bear it ?" asked the Indian, fixing his dark eyes upon the face of the helpless prisoner.

" Yes—yes, I can bear any thing," replied the latter, while his whole appearance gave the lie to his words.

" You are the only prisoner—"

" I know that—I know that."

" Do you remember Colonel Crawford ?"

" Oh Lord ! yes ; and I remember how he died, too."

" Could you bear such a fate ?"

Jenkins' eyes fairly blazed with horror.

" You don't mean—you can not—mean, Monowano, that they intend—to—to torture me—as they did him ?"

The Indian maintained his fixed gaze upon the white-lipped prisoner, without a motion or look that could be taken for an answer.

" Heavenly powers ! Monowano, would they serve me thus ? I have done nothing to deserve such a death. Say ! Do they intend that ?"

Monowano nodded his head forward, as he glided out of the door.

"Let them do it, and be darned! By thunder! I don't care a snap for the whole tribe!"

Strange as it may seem, Jenkins felt exactly what he said. He had reached the utmost bounds of fear, and even passed beyond it. Satisfied now that nothing but death could remain for him, a sort of recklessness seemed to take possession of him, and he was actually freed from fear."

"Yes, sir, I don't care!" he added, talking aloud, yet to himself. "I seen an Injin die at the stake once, singing his own death-song. I'll show these heathen that I can die as well as they can. As they pile on their fagots, and shoot their powder into me, I'll sing Yankee Doodle, and call 'em all the outlandish names I can think of. It would be fine if I could kind of bust loose and run away just then, but I don't believe they'll give me the chance. When the boys up to the settlement hear how Peter Jenkins died, they'll admit he had courage, though I shouldn't wonder if that old Dick Dingle would say I sung Yankee Doodle just to keep my spirits up, and wouldn't have died at the stake if I could have helped myself. But the others will think better."

Jenkins saw the eyes of his captors fixed upon him with a sinister expression. But, as he felt just then, he did not care a whit for their anger, and continued talking as usual:

"Yes; that will be the greatest event in my life—this dying at the stake. I wouldn't mind it at all if it wasn't for the way the fire hurts. Let me see, I wonder if I remember Yankee Doodle."

He bent his head a moment, as if to recall his recollection, and then suddenly burst out:

> "Oh, Yankee doodle, doodle do!
>   Oh! it's Yankee doodle dandy;
> And so Yankee doodle, doodle do,
>   And a doodle dandy.
>
> "So strike the chorus, doodle do,
>   And so doodle dandy,
> So strike the chorus, doodle,
>   And—and so strike the chorus.

"There! I think that will make a grand effect—a great impression. I wish these heathen could only understand the poetry. A great deal of it's original and very impressive. That old chief that I seen die, when I was a boy, I remember mumbled a good deal, and Dingle, who understood his lingo, said he kept talking about himself, praising his own virtues and vices; so I should think it would be a good idea for Peter Jenkins to put his own name in somewhere, just to let these unfeeling wretches know that he thought something of himself."

At this point the prisoner looked up and saw the eyes of the surrounding Indians fixed upon him with much interest. Disregarding the fear which at other times this would have occasioned, he continued:

> "Oh! Peter Jenkins was a great man!
>   Oh! so it's a great man was he;
>   Oh! Peter Jenkins was a great man,
>   Oh, Yankee doodle dandy.

> "He was much greater than General George Washington,
>   Or George the Third, or Dick Dingle, dandy;
>   He wasn't afraid at all to die at the burning, dreadful stake,
>   Doodle dandy.

> "He had an eye like an eagle, and he was very strong,
>   He could run, run could he:
>   A nation mourned him, for he was a nation's loss,
>   A doodle dandy.

> "He slewed a million Injins, and every one was a chief;
>   He teached Daniel Boone how to fight;
>   And he—"

Jenkins, happening to look up at this instant, saw that his Indian guards were much amused at his action and singing. He stopped instantly, unwilling to afford them this pleasure. He dropped into a sullen silence, determined not to utter another sound in their hearing.

" Sing—good—sing!" said one of the savages.

" I know it's good singing as well as you do,' replied Jenkins, who mistook the command for a compliment.

" Sing more—much sing—good," repeated the Indian.

" Oh! you want me to sing, do you? Well, I shan't do it!"

His captors repeated their commands several times, and even threatened violence; but it was useless. One of Jenkins' peculiarities was a most dogged stubbornness; and, when he had determined upon a thing, no human power could change him. He received several kicks and cuffs; but finally his tormentors desisted, evidently wishing to preserve him for the tortures of the stake.

The afternoon wore slowly away, without any thing unusual occurring. A supernatural stillness pervaded the village. Now and then a low, buzzing sound, like the suppressed tones of human voices, could be heard, and occasionally the stoical savages who maintained guard indulged in a guttural word or grunt. But their eyes were never off the prisoner, who finally grew so nervous under their black, snake-like gleaming, that he drooped his head, unable to encounter them.

The feelings of Jenkins, during the last two or three hours, had undergone a great change. The revolting death of the unfortunate Colonel Crawford was constantly before him, and he shuddered to the very soul as he reflected that Monowano had given him to understand the same fate was in store for him. It seemed cruel that Captain Whitley and Dingle should thus desert him in his dire extremity; but reflection told him that in all probability his loss had not been noticed, and an attempt at rescue upon their part, at this late hour, could only result in his own death. There was no Frontier Angel to assist him, and the arm of his truest friend, Monowano, was completely powerless. He doubted not that the noble savage was doing his utmost for him; but, as he had said himself, it was useless to hope in his influence.

When a man is finally brought face to face with death, and is convinced that there is no eluding him—that he is at last in the hands of the Dark Angel—when he is brought to this, we say, there is but one subject that can occupy his mind—the preparation for the last and great change.

The mind of Jenkins was thus engaged when he heard a footstep in the lodge. Looking up he encountered the gaze of Monowano, although he was so transformed that for an instant he failed to recognize him. He was attired in his usual manner, but his face was daubed with the war-paint, so fancifully applied as to give him a most forbidding and frightful appearance. One side of his face was painted perfectly black. Across his forehead were three streaks of blood-red paint, which, dwindling to mere lines at the temples, expanded and were reproduced upon the cheeks, and again upon the upper part of his massive breast. His long black hair was thrown over his shoulders, extending to the waist, in its luxuriant abundance. A head-dress of eagle-feathers, in which the most brilliant colors were visible, arched from the top of his head over upon his back. His nose and ears were without ornaments, and indeed, he never wore any on them. The sides of his face were perfectly regular, devoid of the ungainly cheek-bones, which generally, if not always, characterize the North American Indian. A glance only would give one good reason to doubt whether Monowano was what he pretended to be, so prominent were the Caucasian traits in him.

"What do you wish?" asked Jenkins, looking up from his position.

"You must go with me."

"I am ready, Monowano; but there is one favor that I must ask of you," added Jenkins, thrilling to his soul as he felt that the awful moment had at length arrived.

"What is that," asked the Indian, gently.

Jenkins looked up, and through the disguise of the warpaint, could not fail to see the beaming, pitying heart of the warrior; but it only gave him hope that his request might be regarded.

"Do not let them prolong the torture, as they did with Colonel Crawford. Sink your tomahawk in my brain, when at the stake. You can do it without danger to yourself. Will you?"

Monowano nodded assent.

"And as I am to go with you, cut these thongs. I am so cramped and benumbed that I can hardly move."

Monowano turned and spoke to the other Indians, and then, with several dextrous movements of his knife, freed Jenkins, and lifted him to his feet.

"Wait a moment," said the latter, leaning upon him. "I can't walk; I've got to get the blood moving a little first."

The Indian paused as requested, and in a few seconds Jenkins felt his usual vigor return, with the exception of one leg, which, having been doubled under him, was, as is commonly termed, "asleep." This compelled him to wait some time longer. At first it was as devoid of feeling as a log;

but, as the blood hurried through it, a peculiar, tremulous and not unpleasant sensation was felt, and when he stepped upon it, he drew it up with a gasp, half of pleasure and half of pain.

Monowano noticed these manifestations, and when Jenkins announced he was ready, whispered:

"Walk lame—walk lame; will do you good."

The prisoner looked up in astonishment in the Indian's face; but his gaze was turned away, and it was impossible to divine the expression upon it. Jenkins adopted his suggestion without questioning it.

As they reached the outside, a sight met Jenkins that made him recoil in terror.

"My God! must I go through that, Monowano?"

"Walk lame—walk lame," repeated the Indian, with a singular degree of eagerness.

Extending from the door of the lodge, for over a hundred yards, was a row of men, women and boys, drawn up in a perfectly straight line, all of whom brandished some kind of a weapon. Clubs, knives, hoe-handles, tomahawks and switches were brandished along the line in a manner that showed Jenkins they were only too impatient to apply them to his body. At the further extremity of the line was stationed a half-grown warrior, with the drum ready to give the signal.

"Must I go through this, Monowano?" again appealed Jenkins.

"There is no help, my white friend. If you reach the other end, and have strength, run on into the forest. I will meet you there and assist you. You see there are none but boys and squaws at the other end. But don't talk to me."

Monowano stepped backward and away from the miserable prisoner as he spoke. He made some gesture toward the boy with the drum, who restrained the signal he was about to give. A short consultation was then held with several of the prominent warriors. The result of this was, that every man withdrew from the line, leaving none but the squaws and boys. Jenkins understood at once that Monowano had made a point of his feigned lameness, and secured him this unusual favor. Still, running the gauntlet under the circumstances was enough to break down any man. Jenkins was anxious to start, as he had determined upon the effort hinted at by Monowano.

The latter now approached and said:

"When the drum taps, run, my friend, and make to the thicket yonder—and do not stop!"

Almost at the same instant the drum was heard, and Jenkins bounded away. He had not forgotten to limp, although he made surprising progress. His start was so sudden that he passed the first dozen squaws without a blow. Then several switches stung his back like the sharp scrape of so many needles; and, goaded to madness, he forgot entirely his lameness, and sought only to get over as much ground as possible. Many of the squaws and boys, in their eagerness to get to him, left the line, some following and others stepping in front of him, so that he was shortly surrounded.

One superhuman effort, and Jenkins leaped upward, clean over the heads of his assailants, and bounded away toward the wood, at a terrific burst of speed, the whole pack pouring tumultuously after him.

Jenkins was naturally fleet of foot, and soon distanced the squaws and boys; but he knew there were several warriors upon his track who were capable of greater speed and bottom; and besides, he was unable to maintain, for any time, the velocity with which he was going.

He darted down a sort of declivity into the wood, dodging and darting hither and thither, hoping to elude the eyes of his followers. Unfortunately the forest was open, and it was impossible to effect this. It was now near sunset; but enough light remained to necessitate a longer race than he could maintain.

Exerting himself to the utmost, he soon left the main body of his pursuers behind, but saw that two warriors were gaining at a fearful rate upon him. He knew that as long as there was a chance of securing him alive, the Indians would not fire upon him. Accordingly, he turned all his efforts toward misleading the two savages mentioned. He doubled and changed his course several times, and finally dropped flat upon his face in some briers, hoping and believing his pursuers would pass him unobserved.

Most probably this would have occurred had it not been for

his own imprudence.   The rest thus afforded gave him time
to recover his breath and strength.   From his hiding-place,
he watched his pursuers, as they rapidly neared him.   As they
came closer and closer, his apprehension and confidence in
his own powers increased, until, when within a dozen yards,
and just as they diverged to the left, he sprung to his feet,
and tore away, shouting at the top of his voice.

A shout of exultation announced that the two Indians were
after him, and confident of his recapture.   Hardly knowing
what he did, Jenkins doubled behind a huge towering rock,
while the savages separated, one running around either end,
so as to head off and secure him.   And now took place a most
ludicrous and singular occurrence.

As Jenkins whisked around the corner of the rock, the first
object that met his gaze was nothing less than a huge bear
walking leisurely away from him.   His momentum carried
him nearly against the brute, which wheeled in a great rage
to attack him. Jenkins saw by his open mouth, and the devil
in his eyes, that he was bent on mischief.   Whipping off his
hat, he flung it at his head.   It struck the animal between
his eyes, bewildering him for a moment. During that moment
Jenkins leaped away again, and the Indians made their appearance around the rock, one running directly upon the bear,
which clutched him instantly, and gave him such a hug as to
bring a literal "death halloo" from his red-skinned visage.
One savage, coming thus unexpectedly in collision with a
powerful bear, was hardly prepared for the struggle, and it
required the combined efforts and skill of both to oppose him.

In the mean time, as may be supposed, Jenkins made the
most of this unlooked for advantage.   He saw at once that
his pursuers were engaged with a foe fully worthy of their
steel, and felt some curiosity to know the result of the contest.
He durst not wait, however, but hurried on and was soon safe
from these two Indians at least.

By this time the forest was becoming gloomy and dark,
when, panting and fatigued, Jenkins flung himself upon the
ground and slept like a log.

He awoke late in the night from hearing what seemed to
be the gobble of a turkey very near him.   He was too suspicious to move, and was soon convinced that he was by no

means out of danger. He heard the hooting of owls, the cry of the whippowil, and all manner of voices. The woods appeared to be swarming with his enemies, who were thus signaling to each other.

Fearful that it was near morning, Jenkins determined to make his way out of this labyrinth of perils before it would be too late. Rising to his feet, he cautiously skulked forward, gradually leaving these doleful sounds behind him, and was already beginning to congratulate himself anew, when he suddenly found himself upon the bank of a broad stream.

Here he was taken aback a moment. The faint moon barely afforded a glimpse of the opposite bank, and he felt that his head would be a target for any of his enemies who might be in the vicinity. However, the attempt had to be made, and he commenced wading in, when his attention was attracted by a canoe which was drawn upon the bank a few feet above him.

This he considered fortunate, and without stopping to think of consequences he stepped in, taking the long oar in his hand and using it with more zeal than skill. As the reader has probably learned, Jenkins was most sadly ignorant of these egg-shell concerns, and made but poor progress. When about the middle of the stream, a regular Indian yell, that curdled his blood, broke from the bank he had left, and as a rifle echoed it, he felt the wind of a bullet in his face!

"Lord help me!" he ejaculated, standing on his feet and rowing harder than ever. "Lord help me! this infarnal old thing will be my death yet. I can't make it move at all!"

To his unspeakable terror, the unmanageable canoe commenced going around in a circle, and slowly nearing the shore he had left! Jenkins was fairly frantic, when a second shot whizzed even closer than the first, and a dozen answering yells rung through the forest. Do his utmost, he could make no progress in the right direction.

"Blast the thing!" he exclaimed, in desperation, springing overboard with the intention of swimming to land. To his great joy, he found the water scarcely above his knees. A tremendous splashing followed, and in a moment he was across. He saw that several Indians had entered, and at once plunged into the woods. The darkness here was so great that he felt little apprehension, and continued his flight more leisurely.

"Now catch me if you can!" he muttered. "If you had let me keep my arms, you wouldn't have caught me running like this. No, sir. A dozen of you would have had to bite the dust first."

He diverged at once to the left, so as to place his pursuers at fault. Now and then he paused and listened; but all was still. The soft murmur of the stream, and the gentle rustle of the tree-tops in the night-wind, were all that he heard.

"Doubtless they have gone back, convinced that it is beyond all human power to stop Peter Jenkins when his mind is made up to do a thing. It was my intention to do this all along. I had some idea of waiting till I was tied at the stake, and then walking off in all my dignity. But they dare not follow me. I'd like to see an Injin lay the weight of his hand upon me. O Lord—"

A huge, ball-like body shot toward him, and a grip as if of iron was fastened upon his throat.

"Me got you—me got you!" was uttered in the guttural tones of an Indian.

CHAPTER VII

PROVING THAT A DEAD MAN IS SOMETIMES BETTER THAN A LIVING ONE.

"My heavens, Monowano! you wouldn't kill your old friend, Peter Jenkins, would you?" gasped that person, spasmodically.

The grip loosened at once.

"Monowano mistook his white friend," said the savage.

"I should think you did, the way you grabbed my throat. Who'd you think I was?"

"Let us haste, for they still pursue."

The Indian started forward on a trot, followed by Jenkins, who took pains not to be left behind. Signals were now and then to be heard, but Monowano was too skillful to lead his friend into any trap. They traveled until daybreak through the mountains, when they rested for a time beside a small spring, resuming their journey again ere the sun was fairly above the horizon. The Indian was silent and apparently melancholy, while Jenkins, overjoyed and grateful at his unexpected deliverance, was just the reverse.

"I hear, Monowano," said he, "that you're in love with that gal Maude Burland. She's a fine creature, no mistake; and the first chance I get I'll speak a good word for you."

Had Jenkins seen the glaring look which the Indian turned and gave him as this was uttered, he would probably have said no more; but just then his head was bent downward, watching the toes of his moccasins as he stepped into the tracks of his guide, and he failed to notice any thing unusual in his demeanor, and so he rattled on:

"She's a fine creature, Monowano, and I'll not say to your face but to your *back*, (thunder! that's a good joke,) that she's got a fine feller for her lover. I might have had her once—"

"Ugh! what says my brother?" demanded the Indian, in a voice of thunder.

"O Lord! nothing; why didn't you wait till I had finished what I was going to say. I mean I might have had her once, if she hadn't been so particular as not to like me. She is in love with you; I know it, and now, between you and me, Monowano, don't you love her?"

"The words of my brother are not pleasant in my ears," replied the Indian, with a scowl.

"Oh pshaw! you needn't tell me that, Monowano; I know how a feller feels when he is in love. I have been so several times. I ain't ashamed to own to you (though I wouldn't say as much to Russell Mansfield) that Frontier Angel give me the cramp in the stomach once. But I got bravely over that, and am ready for any thing that turns up. Howsumever, I will say—"

"Hist!" commanded the Indian, crouching suddenly to the earth.

Jenkins did the same and listened intently, but heard nothing. After waiting until his patience was exhausted, he asked, in a suppressed whisper:

"What under the sun is the trouble? I don't hear any thing."

To his consternation, Monowano whirled around as quick as lightning, and drawing his knife, pressed it into his shoulder.

"Good heavens! are you going to kill me?" gasped Jenkins.

"Be dead! be dead!" commanded the Indian. "Be dead! quick! your enemies are upon us!"

Jenkins understood him, and dropped over upon his back and feigned death.

The next minute, full a dozen Indians walked directly up to Monowano. As they came forward, the latter addressed them in the Shawnee tongue, and Jenkins ventured to open the corner of one eye, and take a peep at them. As he caught a glimpse of their savage features, he quickly closed it again.

Knowing it was impossible to fully deceive these warriors, he drew a deep moan, as though he were dying, trusting in the ingenuity of Monowano to carry the stratagem through. The new-comers, however, were not their pursuers, but a portion of a war-party from the Shawnee towns on the Mad river. They had stumbled upon Monowano by accident, without discovering his trail.

Upon seeing the body of a white man, they, of course, questioned him regarding it. He replied that he had overtaken in the forest, and, after wounding, had conquered him, and, if he survived the wound, he intended to take him as a prisoner to Piqua, (another town of the Shawnees.) The Indians evidently were not entirely free from suspicion. Several of them examined Jenkins, rolling him over upon his face, punching him with their rifle-barrels, and making several demonstrations toward scalping him. But Jenkins had learned that his crown was safe so long as Monowano claimed it, as no one would pretend to dispute his right to it.

Another conversation was held, at the close of which the strangers expressed a willingness to accompany the captor and captive to Piqua. Monowano did not expect this, but he was too wily to be taken at fault. Jerking Jenkins to his feet, he assured him, in no gentle tones, that he must now walk, or lose his scalp upon the spot. After much groaning and apparent suffering, he staggered to his feet, and tumbled forward, pitching hither and thither, but, withal, managing to get over the ground at a pretty good pace.

Monowano kept near him, fearful of the treachery of his companions, many of whom cast more than one longing look upon him. Several proposals were made to scalp him, but, of course, this could not be done without the consent of his captor.

Jenkins rather overdid the matter of dying. His continual groaning, limping, and entreaties to kill him outright, were repeated so continually and so similarly, that Monowano saw he was endangering the safety of both. Nearly a mile was passed, when they reached a high, precipitous bluff overlooking the Kentucky river. Here the leader of the war-party demanded a halt and consultation. To guard against the escape of their prisoner, he was carried to within a few yards of the cliff and left, while the warriors retired at a distance where their words could not reach his ears.

Jenkins concluded it was now about time to complete the matter, and give up the ghost entirely. So he drew a long groan, and doubled up, with his face toward the savages. One of the latter walked toward him, examined his pulse, grunted something, and then rejoined his companions. It is hardly to be supposed that Jenkins succeeded in deceiving him, although he afterward affirmed that he did.

By watching the countenances of the Indians, Jenkins believed he could succeed in divining their feelings and intentions, and, as may be suspected, he did not fail to avail himself of this opportunity. He could see that all were opposed to Monowano, who as persistently differed with them. His gestures were earnest, and his course evidently determined upon.

While watching his enemies, Jenkins gradually worked his way backward toward the edge of the cliff, until he felt he was upon the very brink. He then twisted his head (a peculiarity in a *dead man's* conduct that did not escape the eyes of the Indians.) He saw the tops of trees far below him, and rocks and underbrush, while the river itself was many yards distant. This survey finished, he turned his head again toward the council.

Matters were plainly at a crisis. Monowano stood facing he whole war-party, talking and gesticulating rapidly, while their countenances were distorted by the passion of revenge and hate. As he ceased speaking, his opponents conferred hastily together, and then springing simultaneously in the air, brandished their tomahawks and knives, and gave vent to a loud yell of triumph. As quick as thought, Monowano drew his knife, and, with a yell of defiance, sprung backward several feet, so as to stand between Jenkins and his enemies, and here he confronted the dozen enraged warri rs, determined to oppose to death their attempt upon the life of his property.

None of this escaped the individual whose fate was so closely linked with it. Jenkins concluded the time for action had come. If he feigned death longer, it would soon be reality. He saw unmistakably in the manner of the Indians that his scalp had been agreed upon. Rising to his feet, he turned toward the savages, who, at that moment, formed a most interesting and singular tableau. Standing thus, he spoke :

"Fellow-citizens! Peter Jenkins ain't dead! He's alive and kicking! You want his hair, but, by thunder! you shan't have it. Monowano and me have done our best to defend it, but he couldn't do any thing against a dozen cowards, and so I'll have to take the matter in hand myself! And here's the first step toward it!"

As he spoke, he turned and leaped over the cliff!

Had the Indians understood this speech, in all probability they would have interrupted it. But, fortunately, none but Monowano saw his design. His daring leap was so unexpected, that it was not until he disappeared from sight that they comprehended it. They then rushed forward, headed by Monowano, and gazed over. No signs of the white man were seen, nor could they tell where among the trees, rocks and undergrowth he had fallen. Determined, however, not to lose him, the whole pack scattered into the woods, and ten minutes later they were at the bottom of the cliff, searching for the dead or dying man.

After a long time, they found where he had gone through the branches of a tree, and apparently struck the solid face of the rock! But no further traces could be discovered, and the

Indians were finally compelled to the belief that he had miraculously escaped unhurt, and made off in the forest, although the most scrutinizing examination failed to find any trail near where he had struck. Several hundred yards up the bank, however, one of the savages detected a white man's footprints, which, after following fully a half-mile, led into the river, where, of course, it was lost.

Jenkins had resolved upon this leap as a last resort. He bounded outward with his utmost strength, hoping to strike the top of a bushy tree that he had noticed. As he shot through the air and descended with frightful velocity, he experienced that delirious dizziness that thrills a person's frame at such a time, and ever affirmed that it was the most ecstatic moment of his life. He had little hopes of deliverance, but preferred a speedy death to the one which he knew his savage enemies would inflict upon him. But a most wonderful fortune attended this leap for life.

True to his aim, he struck the top of the tree mentioned. As he brushed through the branches he clutched at them, but failed to sustain himself. His fall, however, was broken; and, instead of striking upon the face of the rock, as the Indians supposed, he dropped upon the edge and rolled over. Falling a dozen feet further, his body encountered a rotten tree, whose top leaned against the rock referred to. Down this inclined plane he slid, as if on a sled, and actually bounced over the roots at the base into the cavity behind, shooting through the luxuriant shrubbery, which closed after his passage like a trap-door.

He was so scratched and bruised by this descent as to be unable to rise. Believing himself to be mortally wounded, he concluded to lie still and die at last, without undertaking to prolong life by a flight. The Indians naturally supposed that if he was severely injured he would be found very near the tree through whose branches he first passed; and, if able to run, it was not to be expected he would conceal himself so nigh at hand. This was how they failed to penetrate his leafy retreat. The tree had been blown over years before, and the hollow, formed by its uprooting, was fringed and densely grown over with bushes; so that, unless suspicion led to a careful examination, there was no danger of a discovery.

Jenkins could hear the tramp around him, sometimes coming so close that he was sure he was discovered; then retreating again until he hoped his dying moments would be uninterrupted. His enemies were constantly signaling to each other, in such a manner as to show he was completely surrounded.

He kept his eyes fastened upon the bushes, and at length, through their stalks, detected the shadow of a savage passing to and fro before his hiding-place. It would halt and then again move forward. At length, Jenkins' heart fairly ceased to beat, as the leaves of the bushes parted, and the gleaming face of an Indian appeared set in the opening. The black eyes glowed like coals of fire, and the war-paint made the countenance hideous in the extreme. The glare of the sunshine had so dazzled his vision that for a moment he failed to penetrate the darkness of the hollow. Ere he succeeded in making out the forms of what he saw, a loud yell announced that the trail had been discovered further up the river. The head was instantly withdrawn, and Jenkins heard his hurried footsteps die out in the distance.

"I guess I won't die, after all!" said he, cheerfully, as he realized he was alone. "I don't think it worth while now that they appear to have left me alone. Howsumever, I'll wait awhile before I stick my head out."

Now that the causes which had kept his mind in a fever of tumult were gone, the pain of his wounds made itself felt. He had been switched and banged pretty severely while running the gauntlet, and his original descent of the rotten tree-trunk had in nowise added to his personal comfort. Feeling wretched and miserable, he crawled in beneath the tree as far as he could get, to wait until nightfall before venturing out.

Lying thus, he was just falling into a feverish sleep, when he was electrified by hearing a footstep above him. Not daring to look up, he endeavored to shrink into a smaller compass, and hardly breathed as he listened. A moment after, he heard the bushes pulled aside; then his enemy seemed to halt and gaze down into the cavity. Then came a chuckling noise, and, gracious heavens! he stepped inside. Jenkins shut his eyes and tried to pray, but was interrupted by hearing a well known voice exclaim, as he uttered a suppressed laugh:

"Freeze me to death, if thar ain't that long-legged Jenkins, either gone under, gone to sleep, or took with one of his *faintin'-fits !*"

CHAPTER VIII.

WHICH TREATS OF LOVE

"HALLO, Dingle! where did you come from?" asked 'enkins, in his joy, rising to his feet.

"Oh! I was out on a trail-hunt, on t'other side the river when I see'd them heathen up on the bluff holdin' a confabulation. If my old peepers didn't deceive me, I sec'd Monowano among 'em. They 'peared to be havin' a desprit talk of it, and so I jist shinned up a tree to take observations. Arter a while, I see'd you rise and make a jump, and then kinder understood how things was with you. I see'd you wasn't killed, though you may freeze me if I didn't think you got some scratches. I know'd the redskins would soon be round to hunt you, so I went up stream and paddled over. Some how or other they got into my trail and I had to take to the water again to get cl'ar of 'em. Howsumever, I guess it done you the right turn, as they took it for yours. But come; git out of hyer."

"Ain't there any outside?"

"No; they've left, and the way is cl'ar."

"Have you finished your hunt?"

"Yes; Captain Whitley wanted me to take a run through these parts and see what they thought of his expedition, and find out whether they had any idee of doin' any thing about it."

"Let us go on, then, for I'm tired of staying. Oh! gracious, if I ain't sore."

Jenkins walked with the greatest difficulty, and their progress was necessarily very slow. Dingle was obliged frequently to halt and allow him to rest; but they persevered, and at a late hour in the night the trail-hunters reached the settlement.

Captain Whitley had already disbanded his volunteers, and affairs were moving along in their usual channel. The settlers rightly believed the expedition had checked the outrages of the Indians, for the present at least, and engaged in their customary avocations. The land was cleared, the ground tilled, new cabins erected, and little heed paid to the rumors that occasionally reached them of the indications of a general war along the frontier.

Jenkins' injuries incapacitated him from his duties for a time; but Dingle was constantly employed as scout and ranger, or, as he termed himself, *trail-hunter*, while Jenkins was attended to in Russell Mansfield's family.

Upon the return of the expedition, it reached Mordaunt's ears that Monowano had been caught acting as a spy, and was only allowed to escape death through the urgent entreaties of Dingle. As if to remove what doubts the guardian of our heroine might entertain of this, Jenkins related his account of grappling him during their march through the mountains. But, for all this, he maintained that he was a true friend of the whites.

"He did all he could to save me," said he, "and when he was drove to the last pinch gave me a stick with his knife in the shoulder to make believe he had killed me. Howsumever, that wasn't much."

Upon examination of this wound, it was found that the knife of Monowano had done very little injury, although it had produced a considerable flow of blood. But, in spite of Jenkins' explanations, it awoke grave doubts and suspicion in the minds of many. Jim Peterson, Mansfield and several others believed in the Indian's innocence; but the majority became disaffected. Among the latter was Mr. Mordaunt.

The latter could not be called an unreasonable man. He seldom took a decided step without proper deliberation, and he was never at a loss to give a reason for any of his acts or opinions.

He was a dignified man, who was looked up to by all the settlement, as one who embodied in himself a well balanced heart and head, who would do no man an injury, and whose highest object was to perform his duty in the community in which he moved. He cherished Maude Burland as if she were his own daughter. She was the orphan of Colonel Burland, who, for years, had been his confidant and warmest friend, and who, upon his death-bed, had consigned her to him, under a solemn promise that nothing should be neglected to make her lot as happy as lay in his power.

It was, then, with a great deal of pain that he heard these reports. Wishing to form no unjust prejudice, he examined carefully all that he could glean regarding Monowano. The result of this was a deliberate conclusion that the intercourse between him and Maude ought to be, and a determination that it should be, broken off. The idea of marrying an Indian was always repulsive to him; yet, as long as he had confidence in his honor and uprightness, he interposed no decided objection. His duty to his dead friend, he believed, now demanded that such course should be taken.

Before imparting his resolution to Maude, he desired a calm and unbiased conversation with her regarding it. She was a reasonable girl, and he knew such an interview could be obtained without injury to the feelings of either. When the opportunity presented, he said in a mild manner ·

"Maude, I have long wished a conversation with you Are you willing now to spend an hour or so in speaking upon a subject that much concerns you?"

The tell-tale blood rushed to Maude's face, as her heart told her to what her guardian referred.

"Certainly, father," she replied, using the endearing name of parent, and seating herself near him.

"I wish you to understand, Maude, in the first place, that all which I say will be actuated only by a desire for your welfare and happiness."

"I have never doubted that," she answered, "and my dear, second father must change greatly before I could believe the contrary."

"That is just like you, Maude," added Mordaunt, laying his hand affectionately upon her head. "The guardianship of such a treasure as you, has been the greatest pleasure of my life, and I believe we have understood each other all through. So, without further preliminaries, we will come to the point at once. I believe. Maude, you love Monowano?"

Mordaunt did not look at his ward as he uttered the last question; and yet she dropped her eyes to the floor, and hesitated a moment before replying:

"Yes; I do."

"And he entertains the same passion for you?"

"He does, I believe."

"This attachment has existed for a year?—ever since his visit to the settlement?"

"It has, father."

"Now I shall ask you a question, Maude, to which I wish you to reply as you feel, and only after sufficient deliberation. Do you not believe that, if circumstances demanded it, you could summon sufficient firmness and strength to put away the image of Monowano forever?"

It seemed to Maude as if her heart ceased beating as this question was uttered. Yet, she resolved to meet it fairly, and answer truthfully, no matter what it cost her feelings. Her affection for her guardian excluded the thought of deceit for an instant.

"Should Monowano prove to be a treacherous *Indian*, (the last word was uttered with peculiar emphasis,) my soul would revolt at cherishing my present feelings toward him."

Mordaunt breathed freer, and felt a thrill of pride at this outspoken and honest sentiment.

"The idea of my Maude marrying an Indian has always occasioned me some uneasiness; and yet—"

"But, father, do you *know* that Monowano is an *Indian?*"

"Do you *know* that he is *not?*"

"I have never exchanged a word regarding it; still, I do not *believe* he is."

"There have been numerous surmises and conjectures as to who he could be. Some have affirmed that he is a white man, some a half-breed, while others declare he is an Indian chief, deposed from his authority for some crime. He certainly has many traits peculiar to the white race alone; and, for my own part, I incline to the opinion that there *is* white blood in him. But, whoever he is, I can only consider this uncertainty in regard to him as just ground for suspicion. Ther certainly can be no need of his using deception with *you.*"

"Father, I never should consent to hold a closer relation

to Monowano until I was satisfied in regard to him—until the mystery which hangs about him were cleared away. And, above all, if he proves to be either a full-blooded Indian, or a white man to whose character the least suspicion attaches, *I shall have nothing further to do with him!*"

"Your words, Maude, remove a great load from my mind, and I rejoice to see that you have inherited the decision and energy of mind that always characterized your father. With this uncertainty about Monowano, how came you to sanction his addresses?"

"I will impart to you," resumed Maude, after a pause, "that which is known to no other one in the settlement except myself. I stated, just now, that no words have passed between us in relation to his race or tribe; but, some months since, he gave me to understand that whatever objections either you or I might entertain against him would be removed in less than a year, when the truth in regard to him would be made known. I did not press the subject, although I naturally had a great curiosity to learn more. He added, further, that it was out of his power to impart any thing more than the hint which he had given."

"On these professions, you felt willing to repose confidence in him?"

"On these professions, dear father, I believed Monowano to be an upright and honorable person."

"After hearing what you have told me, I should say no more, were it not for the additional rumors which have reached me since the return of Captain Whitley."

Maude looked up with an inquiring look, as if she did not comprehend him.

"I have made inquiries of all, and much as I dread it, Maude, I must say that I believe Monowano to be a spy and an enemy to us."

He turned toward his ward to see the effect of these words. Her head was still bent, and after waiting in vain for her to speak, he added:

"Yes; I can not avoid this belief. There are not those wanting, however, who believe the contrary; but their belief I look upon as founded solely upon their feelings. Under these circumstances, Maude, I believe that you should no longer notice him."

He half regretted his words, and immediately said:

"I mean, by this, that you should refuse further attentions from him until he is freed from suspicion and reveals himself. What do you think, my child?"

"Your advice is good and I shall follow it."

"Perhaps there could be no harm," resumed Mordaunt, after another pause, "if you should see him and state your decision. It may bring matters to an understanding at once."

"No; I am sure Monowano will tell nothing until the time has expired of which he has spoken."

"He will at any rate understand the cause of your course."

"No, father, I shall not see him. I can see that it is your wish that I should not, although you hope to soften the effect of what you have said. I understand your object, and I guess I have enough respect for my guardian to gratify any wish of his."

She looked up with such a radiant countenance, that Mordaunt embraced her affectionately.

"God bless you, Maude! you are a noble girl; and I am tenfold happier than ever that my confidence in you is strengthened. You have no mother to counsel you, but there is nothing which I can do for you that shall be undone. Go, now, and never forget that you are the daughter of Colonel Mordaunt."

"If you see Monowano," said Maude, rising and hesitating, "you can tell him that I shall not see him until he makes himself known, and the rumors which are circulating of him are explained to all."

"I will do so; I will do so."

Maude departed, and Mr. Mordaunt was left alone. He sat awhile in deep thought, then arose, hummed a tune, drummed upon the panes of the only window in the room, and then, with his hands thrust deep into his pockets, gazed vacantly out upon the settlers at work. Maude was his housekeeper, and he lived alone, having numerous visitors, among whom was their minister, who often held long conversations with him regarding his ward.

Upon the present occasion, Mordaunt seemed to be discussing some question in his mind, and to have considerable difficulty in arriving at a conclusion. It was not until a good half-hour had elapsed that he muttered, "It will be the safest plan, after all," and putting on his hat, left the house.

He called upon several of the most prominent men in the settlement, and held conversations with them. He requested the commander of the block-house to instruct the sentinels to prevent Maude leaving the village at night. The commander promised that his wish should be regarded, and Mordaunt felt considerably relieved. He next told Dingle, and the others who sometimes acted in the capacity of scouts, to ask Monowano to visit the village, and call upon Mordaunt, who wished to have some conversation with him.

The half-hour's debate with himself, of which we have spoken, was caused by the hesitation of Maude's guardian in taking these steps, after her promise to him. It seemed as if ne were doing her injustice. It was not because he had the slightest doubt of her intention that he did this, but because he had some lingering fears of her resolution. The information regarding the supposed Indian, which had been imparted by her, set him upon a new train of thought; but, strive as much as he might, he could not entirely free himself of the dislike he felt against Monowano. A frank, outspoken man himself, he could not bear any thing that bordered upon cautiousness or mystery, and it was impossible to persuade himself that Monowano could have any just reason for wrapping himself up in such doubt and uncertainty.

Satisfied now that all possible precaution had been taken, and that all would be well, he gave himself no further trouble regarding our heroine. He busied himself with the affairs of the settlement, in which he took great interest, and which so occupied his mind that he paid little heed to the actions of the gentle being under his charge.

The second night after the interview which we have recorded, Maude was returning through the settlement to her home. She had spent the evening with a lady friend, and was busily occupied with the thoughts which it produced, when she suddenly started as she heard the signal of Monowano—the cry of the whippowil. She involuntarily paused, as if he had suddenly appeared before her; and was about to move on, when she recalled the words of Mordaunt in which he had advised her to see him and explain matters. It seemed the best course; and, halting but a moment, she turned her steps toward one of the gates. A few moments brought her to it, and she looked up expectantly for the sentinel to open it and allow her to pass.

"Can't do it, Miss Maude. Sorry, but I've been forbidden."

She looked up in amazement.

"Why is this? Is there unusual danger?"

"No; I don't know as there is; but *no one* can pass these gates after sundown, unless the boss says so."

"Such have been the commands all along; but they never affected me before, and why should they now?"

"All I've got to say, Miss Maude, is, that that's the orders, and you are surely not the one who would seek to divert a sentinel from his duty."

She felt the rebuke in these tones, and without speaking further, turned toward her home. But she was considerably excited by the words of the sentinel, and was partly at a loss to account for them. She felt unwilling to believe her guard ian had exercised this unusual surveillance upon his part; but she was finally compelled to the belief. It wounded her feelings to think he should deem such a course necessary, after she had given him her word; and, for the first time in her life, she believed her guardian had acted unjustly by her.

She saw him as she entered her home, but said nothing of what was uppermost in her mind. After she retired, she once more heard the faint and plaintive call of Monowano. She listened intently, until a late hour, but heard no more, and finally fell into a sweet and dreamless sleep.

Affairs in the settlement moved on as usual for several days. Nothing more was heard of the Indian Monowano, and Mr. Mordaunt reasonably hoped that he would remain away for the future. Dick Dingle was absent up country on one of his trail-hunts, and Jenkins had so rapidly recovered from his injuries that he calculated on joining him upon his return. The recent expedition against the Indians proved a most wholesome proceeding; for reports came from Tennessee that their depredations had ceased, for the time being at least; and, in the immediate vicinity of the village, scarcely a sign of an Indian had been seen since their return.

One warm, pleasant afternoon, about a month after the

Interview between Mordaunt and Maude, the latter emerged from the settlement, intending to take a short ramble through the adjoining wood. There could be no danger or impropriety in such a step, as the wood was full of choppers, and the clear ring of their axes, and the shouts of their lusty voices came like sweet music from every part of the forest. The knowledge of their proximity could but inspire courage in the faintest heart. Each browny wood-chopper swung his gleaming ax within a step of his loaded rifle; and it was impossible for such a band to be taken by surprise.

Maude wandered aimlessly forward, the balmy afternoon filling her with a languid indifference as to whither she turned her steps. The clear, azure sky overhead, the hazy atmosphere resting lazily on wood and river, the soft, musical ripple of the stream against its bushy banks, all conspired to increase this feeling of delicious languor. In a dreamy forgetfulness she walked forward, paying no heed to her footsteps, until a feeling of fatigue induced her to seat herself upon the fallen trunk of a tree. Seated thus, she commenced examining a number of flowers she had culled by the way, with a listlessness that disregarded what was passing around her. It was not until she heard a voice that she turned her startled gaze to her left, and saw standing before her—Monowano!

It would be difficult to describe the emotions visible upon the face of the Indian. He was arrayed in his hunting-costume, and his appearance, at the moment Maude looked up, was such as to prepossess the most casual observer. His dress was arranged with taste, and totally free from that gaudy excess of ornament so characteristic of the American Indian. His dark eye had lost its eagle keenness, and the predominant expression of his face was that of reproachful sadness.

"Why, Monowano! I did not think it was you!" exclaimed Maude, in astonishment.

The Indian made no reply, but continued his quiet, reproving look, until Maude, out of embarrassment, added:

"Is this meeting accidental upon your part, Monowano?"

"The call of the whippowil has been heard in the wood, but the Evening Star has failed to beam upon him."

Maude understood plainly the meaning of this, and her heart beat quicker as she resolved within herself to impart to him all that had passed between her and her guardian. But, as she was about to speak, her courage failed her and she only said :

"My father wishes to see you, in the village."

"The heart of the white man is deceitful, and Monowano's shadow will no more darken their threshold."

"Monowano," repeated Maude, in a reproachful tone, and heightening in color, "my father is not deceitful."

"Monowano has been upon the war-path; he has struck for his white brothers; and, when the arm of the Shawnee has been raised, he has seized the knife, and the blow has fallen harmless. And for this the white man seeks his life."

This was the first direct reference the Indian had ever made to the suspicion which many of the settlers held against him. For a moment Maude was at a loss to reply.

"Your life is sacred in the village," and, gathering courage as she proceeded, the maiden continued : "I have heard the call of the whippowil, and sought to come to you, but was prevented. I had, however, promised my father that I should not see you, and I am now about to give the reason."

The Indian stood as motionless as a statue, and Maude, not daring to encounter his gaze, recommenced :

"There is a mystery about your movements as well as about yourself which justly creates this suspicion. And the refusal upon your part to disclose to me—"

At this unlucky moment Maude chanced to look up, and saw, not ten feet behind Monowano, the figure of Pete Jenkins surveying them both with an air of mischievous drollery. He seemed to have come upon them by accident, and was waiting now to see their actions for his own amusement, not sensible that he could hurt the feelings of those whom he was watching. The Indian saw that something behind him had attracted the attention of the speaker, and instantly turned and confronted the grinning Jenkins.

"Why is this?" asked Monowano, laying his hand upon the buckhorn handle of his knife, and surveying him fiercely.

"Oh, now, you needn't appear so mad about it," said Jenkins, waving his hand with the air of a father. "I've suspected this all along, and won't laugh at you. So, just go ahead with your love-making, and don't let me bother you. I'll look on."

So saying, he complacently seated himself upon the log beside Maude, and awaited her movements.

"I am not aware that this meeting is for your benefit," said the latter, haughtily, rising and preparing to move toward the village. As she reached Monowano, she said, in a low tone, but loud enough to be heard by Jenkins: "I will see you again, and explain what I wish to."

The Indian merely glanced at her, and then turned silently on his heel, and disappeared in the forest.

"I'll be derned if that ain't mean," said Jenkins, indignantly. "I come out on purpose to see them perform, and both have gone off without obliging me. Never mind; I'll tell her father, to pay for this."

CHAPTER IX.

A NIGHT OF EVENTS.

TRUE to his word, Jenkins related to Mr. Mordaunt all the particulars of the interview which he had witnessed, laying great stress upon the parting sentence of Maude, in which she promised to see Monowano again.

"Oh, my gracious! but they were loving as a couple of doves. You oughter seen 'em!"

Perhaps the rebuff which Jenkins had received tended somewhat to an exaggerated color in his narration. At any rate, Mordaunt's idea of the interview was far from the truth.

It caused him great uneasiness, to say the least. He saw that it was simply impossible to prevent any number of meetings between Monowano and his ward. While he had full faith in her intentions, he felt that her surroundings were such as to overrule them; and he well feared that the fatal infatuation would some day lead his child to take her departure forever from his roof. He spent several days in thinking carefully upon the matter; and more than once he consulted long and earnestly with the minister and several of his most intimate friends.

The result of these deliberations was a rather startling

determination upon his part. He resolved to return east again, and, by making his home in the thickly-settled portions of the country, place his ward forever beyond the reach of Monowano's visits. Within the pale of civilization, he felt sure she would soon learn to blush at the passion of her youth, and to abhor the sight of the one who was now so dear to her.

When such a man as Mr. Mordaunt settled upon some plan, it was not long before he acted upon it. Two weeks from the interview of which we have spoken, he was ready for starting. He had engaged a dozen men to accompany him as far as Pittsburg, where he was to be left with Maude. Two boats were provided, in each of which were six men, well armed and provisioned, and who were to take to the river at the settlement, and by means of their oars reach Pittsburg. The leading boat was guided by Mr. Mordaunt himself, while six strong, vigorous men were to take their turn at the oars as the occasion demanded. In the other boat, besides Maude, were also six men, including Jenkins. Mordaunt sought to obtain Dingle, but the commander of the block-house felt that the scout could not be well spared from the settlement at such a time. The traveler, therefore, was compelled to start upon the perilous journey without him. Maude, however, was provided with a strong and formidable body-guard; and, as every soul was experienced in the dangers of a frontier life, Mordaunt felt that the greatest difficulty to overcome was that of the severe labor required of his men.

The boats were long and narrow. Upon each was constructed a sort of rude cabin, which, besides sheltering their arms and provisions, afforded a retreat for all in case of being overtaken by storm. In the rear boat was an apartment sacred to the use of Maude herself, into which none ever intruded, and where she was allowed to pass her nights without being disturbed by the others.

Mordaunt had stated to his ward, long before, his intention of returning east and remaining there. He professed to be wearied of the wilderness life, and to long once more for the comforts and society of civilization. She seemed glad of this decision upon his part, and willingly consented to accompany him before he had expressed any wish to that effect.

Every thing, then, being in readiness, on a clear morning,

In the autumn of this year, our little fleet started hopefully up the Ohio. There were pleasant adieus exchanged between Maude, Mr. Mordaunt and the settlers; but most of the latter understood that the farewell was not final, as their friend had promised to return when his ward *was married and settled down in life.* As the boats were shoving off from the shore, Jim Peterson remarked, half jokingly, to Mr. Mordaunt:

"I don't know whether you ought to take that ar' Jenkins along with you or not. Ef thar's any redskins about, he'll be sure to get thar paws upon him. Dingle, you know, give him up twice, when he's been in thar hands."

"But didn't I get out *myself*," called out Jenkins, who had heard the remark, "and without any help ?"

"Yas, that's the fact, Jenkins; but be careful and don't get any of them *faintin' fits* of yourn, when things look squally."

Jenkins shook his head menacingly, as the boats swept out into the middle of the stream. The men bent to their oars, and their long, steady pulls sent them swiftly and gracefully up the gleaming Ohio.

In less than an hour the two boats were hidden by a bend in the river, and the settlement returned, in a great measure, to its usual appearance. The settlers naturally felt some anxiety in regard to the adventurers, but their experience and wisdom made all confident in their ability to reach their destination in safety. Not a *word* of fear passed between the adventurers as they saw the village which had sheltered them so long disappear in the distance.

Mordaunt, fully sensible of the dangers incurred by this undertaking, took every precaution for safety, and made every preparation in his power for any emergency. Two of his men had good knowledge of the Ohio, and, under their direction, he kept his boat constantly in the channel, the other remaining but a few yards in the rear. They had resolved not to run in to shore, unless it was at some settlement or fort where there could be no possibility of incurring danger.

Before leaving, it had reached the ears of several men, including Mr. Mordaunt, that the Indians through whose country they were now journeying were unusually hostile, and there was every appearance of a general war breaking out along the frontier. This was the principal reason for using such extraordinary caution, although it was kept from the ears of Maude.

The first day passed without any thing unusual occurring. The weather continued pleasant until late in the afternoon, when there were signs of a storm. The night set in dark and cloudy, and was moonless and cold. No rain fell, but the wind could be heard whistling drearily through the forest. The men pulled powerfully and steadily, and conversed only now and then in low tones. They had now a long distance to pass—several hundred miles—where the shore was totally devoid of any signs of civilization. Many miles above, they would reach a sparsely settled country, while a long distance behind lay their own village, which now seemed doubly dear as they were deprived of its comforts and shelter.

The prow of the boat which held Maude now and then touched the stern of the one ahead, as the inmates felt a natural desire to be in as close company as the circumstances would permit. Mr. Mordaunt carefully guided his own, his eyes flitting from side to side; and, as the dark line of the shore came to view, he cautiously steered away from it until all was wrapped in impenetrable darkness again. Now and then he admonished those in the rear to be careful and not lose his company, and it required no adept to see that he was fully sensible of the responsibility of the situation which he held.

Early in the evening, the men had taken a rest of a couple of hours' duration, during which their evening meal had been partaken, and they had indulged in the last cheerful conversation of the journey. Reinvigorated, and anxious to press onward, they were now rowing with deep and muffled oars. The soft ripple of the ashen blades served only to make the stillness more profound.

"It's getting late I'm thinking, Miss Maude," said one of the men, who was enjoying his breathing spell, "and Mr. Mordaunt, I guess, would like to have us all sleep when we can."

"Oh! I am not sleepy," replied our heroine, as though aroused from some revery. "I could not sleep should I lie down. There is something in the stillness around us that prevents it."

"I hope Miss Maude is not alarmed."

"Why do you hope so?" she asked, suddenly turning her head toward the man who had addressed her. The latter, somewhat embarrassed, replied:

"Why because — because I should be sorry to hear it, Upon such a journey as this, we all want our courage around us."

"Have you yours?" asked Maude, in the same pointed manner.

"I believe I've as much as any one," replied the man, in a blustering manner.

"Careful, and not too loud there!" admonished Mordaunt, turning his head toward them.

"And I believe *I* have as much as any one," added Maude, in a lower tone but with the same directness; "yet I am not ashamed to own that this dreadful gloom chills me to the very heart."

"It is better than daylight, Miss Maude; in such darkness as this, the gleaming eye of a Shawnee can not cut the air; and even Sime Girty with all his imps might be watching for us, and we rub his nose without his seeing us."

"By thunder! I'm scar't!" said Jenkins, in a sepulchral voice, from his position within a few feet of the speakers. Maude started at his unnatural tone and asked:

"Why, what has frightened you?"

"Oh blazes! just look how dark it is. We might run onto a whole fleet of Injin canoes without knowing it. I wish I'd stayed home, instead of coming in this derned old thing."

"Why did you come then?" asked our heroine, in a reproving tone.

"'Cause I was a fool; that's why! No, it wasn't either. I came out of pure love for you, my dear Maude. There's only one thing that makes me feel uneasy just now."

"And what can that be?"

"If the Injins only *should* get us, I'm afeard they'd be desprit mad on account of my running away from them, when they had me before. I don't know but what it would have been best if I'd stayed with them, and settled down into their life."

"You *are* the most outrageous fool I ever met!" said the first speaker, in disgust at this evidence of timidity.

"Who's a fool, I'd like to know?" demanded Jenkins, in great indignation, and pitching his voice to a high key.

"Let me hear no more of that loud talking," commanded Mordaunt, in a threatening manner.

This checked the conversation for a time. But the stillness and gloom seemed to oppress all so much that it was a relief to hear each others' voices. At length, Jenkins ventured, rather timidly, again:

"I wonder if the men ahead know where they are going, when it is black as a wolf's mouth around them."

"Of course they do. They are going up the Ohio."

"I expect they are; but how are they to keep from running in to shore and right onto a nest of the heathens?"

"Their common sense will prevent that—"

"What is that long, shadowy line that is yonder on our left?" asked Maude, in a lower tone.

"There's the shore, now!" exclaimed Jenkins. "Hello, Mr. Mordaunt! look out! look out! you'll be in among 'em 'fore you know it."

Mordaunt was heard to speak in a low tone to his men, and the next minute the canoes were side by side.

"See here, Jenkins," said he, in a guarded but meaning voice. "This is the second time I have cautioned you to preserve silence, and it is the last time! If any thing will bring us into peril it will be your imprudence; and the next time I am obliged to speak to you, you shall be taken in to shore and left there!"

"I only spoke for your own good," muttered Jenkins, as his canoe again fell behind.

"And he only spoke for your good," added one of the men, meaningly. "It'll save you some trouble if you'll remember what was said, for Mr. Mordaunt never threatens in sport."

This once more effectually checked conversation for the time; but, as the subdued murmur of voices could be heard in the front boat, Jenkins concluded there was no danger of Mordaunt carrying out his appalling threat, so long as he exercised ordinary precaution in conversation.

"If we only had Dingle along I shouldn't feel half so scar't. He knows all about Injins, and could tell where they were even on such a dark night as this."

"He must be rather smarter than you generally find people," remarked one of the men, somewhat nettled at this slur upon the present company.

"Of course he is," replied Jenkins, confidently. "He wouldn't care if you did talk out loud on such a night as this; 'cause why, he wouldn't go so near that they could hear us."

"And how would he prevent it, I should like to know."

"Why easy enough," replied Jenkins, rather louder than was prudent; and, recollecting himself, he added in a meaning whisper, "He'd *smell* 'em! Dingle can smell the Shawnee half a mile off."

A scornful laugh was the only reply.

"You needn't laugh, for it's true. I've known him to do it."

"He's ahead of you, then, is he not? It seems you have managed to fall into their hands several times."

"And fall out again *myself*," quickly and proudly retorted Jenkins.

"Sh! Heaven save us! What is that?" asked Maude in a hurried whisper, laying her hand upon his arm. He started, as if stung by an adder, and looked up stream. On a point of land which seemed to project into the river was a large fire burning, which, coming into view all at once, showed that they had just swept around a bend in the stream.

"That's them!" said Jenkins.

"What of it? Don't make a fool of yourself. If you make a noise all will now be lost."

Mordaunt suffered the two boats to fall side by side, and said:

"Yonder is a most dangerous point to pass. The light from the fire strikes far out into the river, and a little imprudence upon our part will send them out after us. I forbid a single word passing between you, until we have left them far behind. Keep directly beside us, dip your oars carefully, and all will be well."

The two boats now neared the dreaded point in almost perfect silence. The suppressed ripple of the muffled oars, and the deep-drawn respiration of the laborers, were all that told of the passage of a boat up the Ohio.

The blazing fire was watched with the most intense interest. There was no doubt of its character. A large war-party of savages were congregated there, without the least fear of disturbance from any foes. Now and then a dark figure flitted to view, and the branches and trunks of two trees reflected the red glare of the flames, while behind them all was solid darkness. Soon the sound of voices could be heard as though the Indians were rejoicing over the success of some foray against their enemies. Mordaunt saw to his dismay that the light of the fire reached nearly if not entirely across the river, and while crossing this gleaming band they would be exposed to any glance that chance or design might throw in that direction.

There was no alternative, however, and they moved steadily onward.

"Just look!" whispered Jenkins. "You can see a *thousand* of 'em stretched out around the fire."

No reply was made, as all were too intent upon the frightful duty before them. As they came nigher and nigher, numerous forms could be distinguished, some stretched at full length, others sitting, and many smoking and chatting. They were certainly a formidable body, and their careless, noisy laughter showed they were fully sensible of this fact.

As the belt of light was reached, the rowers instinctively dropped their oars deeper, and sent the boat shooting rapidly forward. At this instant one of the Indians passed between the blaze and the river, and his grotesque and gigantic shadow quivered over the trembling whites. The hearts of the rowers throbbed as, at the same second, they noticed an alarming fact. They had unconsciously approached so close to the shore opposite the war-party, that the ends of the oars on one side of their boats swept the mud from the bottom.

"Further to the right! further to the right!" whispered Mordaunt, sheering his own boat into deeper water. The second attempted to follow, but suddenly stuck in the soft mud, and the oars with a loud plash dashed the spray over the inmates. They were in the brightest part of the lightest portion, and Maude glanced toward the shore. No yells showed that they were discovered, but there was an unusual commotion among the Indians, and either fancy or her sense of hearing told her that they were launching their canoes.

While this was taking place she felt her own boat moving

again. One of the men had sprung overboard, and applying his Herculean shoulder to the stern of the canoe, sent it shooting forward as he sprung into the stern and added his own impetus to its motion. A moment later and both boats were side by side in the darkness again.

All drew a breath of relief, and for a time not a word was exchanged. The oars were dipped with unusual caution, and the most intense listening failed to detect any sounds of pursuit. Were their enemies searching for them, they were using the same stealth. This could hardly be expected, under the circumstances, as the Indians could have had no time to make any preparations.

More than once the dark outline of some jutting point of land was taken for the dreaded canoes of their enemies, and in the most breathless suspense they rowed by them, into the deeper gloom beyond.

It was not until several miles had been passed that the whites ventured to congratulate each other upon their fortunate escape.

"Do you suppose we were seen?" asked Maude.

"Of course we were," replied one of the men.

"How was it that they gave no signs, and made no attempt at pursuit?"

"They were not sure who we were, and knowing nothing of our numbers and strength, must have concluded that the risk was too great to attack us in this darkness."

"Thank Heaven for the darkness then!" said Jenkins, venturing to speak once more.

"Maude, are you up yet?" asked Mordaunt, in a reproving tone, allowing her boat to come beside his.

"Yes, father, I surely could not sleep at such a time."

"This is imprudent, exposing yourself thus. This night air is dangerous, without taking into account the other dangers that threaten. It is my wish that you should retire at once."

"Shwish!" admonished one of the men, cautiously. All eyes were turned ahead—and there, slowly approaching through the gloom, could be distinguished the shadowy outlines of a flat-boat.

"A decoy of the Indians!" whispered Jenkins.

The flat-boat was directly upon them, and only a dextrous use of the oars prevented a collision.

"Hello there! Indians!" called out a voice, as the larger vessel came alongside. The bustle of preparation was heard, when Mordaunt called out:

"We are friends! Don't be alarmed!"

"Who are you, and where bound?" asked a man, his head appearing above the gunwale.

"White men like yourselves; we are bound for Pittsburg. What is your destination?"

"Down to the settlements below. How are the Injins?"

"Pretty troublesome; keep a sharp look-out. We passed a large party several miles down the river. Look out for decoys."

"We are all right. Horace Mordaunt, don't you know the man you're talking to."

"I've heard the voice before, but can not recognize it just now."

"You don't suppose *Simon Kenton* is to be catched napping do you?" asked the speaker, in a pleasant, musical voice.

"Ah, Kenton, is that you. I'm glad of it; your presence will be the salvation of the party. How is the country above that we must pass through."

"Pretty bad—pretty bad, I must tell you. We've had three brushes with the thieves. Howsumever, keep a bright look-out, and if you get through to-morrow night without being stopped, you'll stand a good chance of seeing Pittsburg. Good-by, all of you."

"Good-by!" returned several voices to the well-known ranger.

The men had kept their boats stationary during this hurried conversation, and the flat-boat was now floating away from them and fading in the darkness. In a moment, it had disappeared altogether, and our friends were left to continue their journey.

It was now near midnight, and Mordaunt concluded to give his men several hours' rest. One or two proposed to run in to shore and pass the time quietly upon the bank; but the majority decided this would be too dangerous an attempt, and a direct violation of the vow they had taken never to land until they saw their safety demanded it, or until it was the will of their leader and themselves. Accordingly, a couple of rude anchors were dropped gently to the bottom, and preparations were made for the rest they so much needed.

A man stood guard in each boat, who was to be relieved at the end of two hours. Mordaunt took the duty of sentinel for his own, and an experienced backwoodsman the same for the other. Jenkins, feeling little inclination for sleep, was allowed to keep his friend company. Thus the two boats rested on the silent surface of the Ohio. The soft, almost inaudible ripple of the current as it gently washed the prow, the mournful wailing of the night-wind through the wilderness along the shore, and the whispered words of the watchful sentinels, were the only sounds that the listening ear could have detected. Mordaunt had once more stated to Jenkins that any imprudence upon his part would be punished by landing and leaving him upon the bank, so that the fellow had enough to keep him silent.

Once or twice a plashing was heard on the Kentucky side, as though a person stepped in the water, and then out again. Mordaunt was at first disposed to believe it nothing more than a dipping limb or root, or perhaps the wash of the stream against a rock or stone. But the sound was such that at length it alarmed him, and made him apprehensive that some mischief was brewing near him. After listening awhile, and vainly endeavoring to satisfy himself in regard to it, he gently touched the man beside him. The latter had once been a captive among the Indians, and was much skilled in their wiles and stratagems.

"Listen !" whispered Mordaunt, in answer to the inquiring look he made as he opened his eyes. The man did so, and Mordaunt asked:

"What do you make of it, Pedro ?"

"Some deviltry, I'm afeard. It might be a bear or some varmint craunchin' something 'long the shore, but more likely it's some the heathen conjurin' up some contrivance for our benefit."

"What could they possibly be doing, Pedro ?"

"Like enough they haven't canoes, and they're fixing up some logs to float out to us on. Ef I might venture a little advice, captain, I'd say, dig out of these parts as soon as convenient."

"It shall be done at once. Pete there! (to the second sentinel) wake your men, and we'll be off. Let them handle their oars carefully."

All was accomplished, and, in a short time, the two boats were again making their way up stream. They had gone perhaps a hundred yards, when Jenkins shouted loud enough to be heard several miles away:

"Lord save us! I seen an Injin then right beside us."

"Where? where?" asked several men, grasping their weapons.

"Right out there—swimming in the water, only a yard or two off. He just dove. There he is again! Don't you see his head?" Right out there!"

The dark, ball-like head of an Indian was seen moving on the surface, and in an instant several rifles were pointed at it.

"Hold! don't more than one fire!" commanded Mordaunt. "Wait till we see the danger. One of you shoot that Jenkins if he bawls in that manner again. We saw the savage in this boat before he did. I will attend to him when he rises, and all of you keep your eyes open for other danger!"

At this moment the water parted, and the head of the savage rose to view not ten feet away. Mordaunt had his rifle at his shoulder and his aim upon him when he spoke.

"Don't shoot! It is Monowano; no one else is near!"

Mordaunt lowered his rifle in amazement, and the next instant the Indian was floating alongside.

"What brings you here, Monowano? Get in the boat," said Mordaunt, greatly gratified at his happy disappointment.

"No, Monowano will swim," replied the mysterious being, in a voice which would have betrayed to a practiced ear a slight feeling of coldness and *hauteur;* but the next instant it changed to a more friendly tone, and he replied, as he floated gracefully upon his back without the least visible effort.

"The path to the white man's home in the east is long, and the Shawnees are watching in the bushes! The path that leads back is shorter, and the bushes hold few enemies."

A suspicion of the Indian's object flashed across the mind of Mordaunt, and he replied gently but firmly:

"That can not be, friend Monowano; we must go on. But do we encounter *great danger?*"

" The panther crouches in the tree-tops, the bear has scented the trail, and the rattlesnake is coiled in the path; but the eye of the Shawnee is sharper than the panther's, and the knife is deadlier than the sting of the rattlesnake !"

" O Lord! let us go back !" fairly shouted Jenkins. " Get in this old boat, Monowano, and steer us back."

" Monowano has spoken."

" Do you think—"

But Mordaunt saw the Indian had gone, and would not return. He did not finish his sentence, but said:

" Row in to shore."

" I say, captain," muttered the man known as Pedro, " if that bawling Jenkins is to go any further, _I_ get out and go back."

" What are you going in to shore for ?" demanded Jenkins, a frightful suspicion crossing his mind. Mordaunt made no reply, and he continued :

" I know what you're up to. You're going to leave me. Murder! help! thieves! Good Shawnees! come down and help me !" he shouted, in the most vociferous tones. The men only rowed the faster.

" Help! help! I'll turn renegade just as sure as you leave me! I'll be worse than Simon Girty or Tom McGable! I'll bring a force down against Pittsburg and burn you all at the stake! Derned if I don't !"

His threats only added an impetus to the labors of the men. All were anxious to rid themselves of one who, in all probability, would prove their destruction should he remain.

" This is confounded mean! I sha'nt stand it! I won't holler any more, if you let me stay ! Murder! help! quick! I'll be hanged if I don't bring the whole tribe down upon you," he added, turning and speaking rapidly to those beside him. It was useless. The men had made up their minds.

Maude was watching this proceeding with the most painful interest. She regretted the step, but her own sense told her the safety of all demanded it, and she did not venture to remonstrate.

" You'll be sorry for this !" said Jenkins, as he distinguished the shore. " I won't forget it. When you all get catched and are burning at the stake, you'll think of it, see if you don't. Help! MURDER !"

The last exclamation was uttered in tones loud enough to wake the dead, and just as the boat touched the bank.

"Come, out with you," said one of the rowers. "Out with you before you're thrown out! You've been warned enough, and this is your own fault."

Jenkins saw the men were determined, and after some whimpering, stepped ashore.

"*Murder!* MURDER! MURDER!"

He exerted himself so much in uttering these words, and opened his mouth so wide, he was obliged to close his eyes for a time. When he opened them again, there was nothing to be seen of the two boats! He was alone in the most dangerous part of the country belonging to the hostile Indians!

CHAPTER X

SURROUNDED BY DEATH.

AFTER ridding themselves of Jenkins' dangerous presence, the two boats rowed rapidly up the river, and, in a few moments, were in the center of the stream again. His startling cry of "Murder!" was heard, and all was still. Finding his cries could accomplish nothing, Jenkins in all probability had turned his thoughts to his new situation, and prudently restrained his exhibitions of rage.

"It seems a pity to leave him thus!" said Maude, who, during this proceeding, had made her appearance. "Will it not be his death?"

"Fudge! no; he'll make his way back to the settlement in short order, while if we had kept him, our hair would not have been our own by to-morrow's light. It's a good riddance."

"But he threatened—"

"Ha! ha! Maude, that was the best part of the joke. He threaten! I should like to see Pete Jenkins carrying out his threats."

Maude said no more, but retired to her apartment, where

she lay a long time thinking deeply upon what had passed—not so much upon Jenkins' adventure as upon the singular appearance of Monowano. After departing from the settlement as secretly as they could, and under the belief that that Indian was far away in the wilderness at the time, he had most suddenly shown himself at midnight, swimming beside them in the river, and as suddenly disappeared.

Before going, however, he had uttered a warning, and one of dreadful portent. She had heard his words, and knew they were not meaningless. Despite herself, a dark suspicion of treachery crossed her mind. The mystery that hung around this Indian, she feared was but a deep-laid scheme upon his part to accomplish some design against the settlement. His advice for them to turn back had an air of suspicion upon its very face. It was known they had left a formidable band of their enemies behind, and it would certainly be a daring proceeding to encounter them again. It cost Maude Burland great misery to think thus of one for whom she still had a strange love, but the words of older and wiser ones compelled her to. Her heart shuddered as she reflected upon the journey that was yet before them. A chilling presentiment of evil hung constantly about her. Her only relief was in constant supplication to the One who alone could save them; and, with a prayer still upon her lips, she fell asleep.

When she awoke the sun was high in the heavens, and a day of rare beauty was upon them. On either hand the tall, luxuriant trees lined the stream, while the exuberant bushes dripped and nodded in the cool current. A deep, almost *audible* stillness reigned about them, and the sublimity of the mighty solitude was felt in all its vastness. Here and there a depression or swell gave an idea of the almost interminable wilderness which surrounded them. Overhead several birds were circling, and their joyous call could be heard from different parts along the shore.

But not a sign of human life, besides their own presence, could be seen. Civilization had passed beyond this point, which yet awaited the ax of the woodman and the plow of the husbandman. And yet our friends well knew that that forest, stretching around them in all its solemn stillness, was not devoid of human beings. In it the red-man lurked, and the crack of his rifle, the crash of his tomahawk, were sounds that often broke the sylvan quiet of the woods.

A brisk breeze was blowing up stream, and a couple of rude sails on each boat carried them steadily along without the aid of oars, so that all were now enjoying a lengthy resting-spell. Some of the men were sleeping, others chatting and admiring the beautiful scenery through which they were passing. The air and morning were so exhilarating that it was impossible for them to resist the influence. The terrors of the past night were forgotten; all were hopeful and joyous.

The favorable wind propelled them finely until noon, when, to their joy, a flat-boat was descried far up the river A thought of treachery crossed the minds of several at first, but it was soon certain they were friends. There appeared some confusion and alarm upon the flat-boat for a time, but its inmates soon seemed satisfied, and manifested considerable anxiety to meet their brothers.

There is nothing that will bring two strangers together so quickly as a sense of impending danger to both. A feeling of brotherhood is awakened, more especially when the new acquaintances are of the same nation; that makes them friends at once.

In a few moments the two boats were anchored alongside, and conversing in the most social manner. Almost the first question was sure to be:

"How are the Indians?"

"Pretty troublesome," replied Mordaunt. "We saw a large company last night. If you can elude them, the most dangerous point will have been passed by that time. How are they above?"

"Bad—very bad!" replied one of the men on the flat-boat, impressively. "You will have to run the gauntlet to-night."

"Did they attempt any thing against you?"

"They made no open attack, because they saw we were well prepared. But more than one treacherous shot was fired. Large numbers could be seen skulking along through the trees, and the only thing that saved us was our strength."

" Do you believe we will be attacked ?"

"I must say that the prospect is that way. I can only admonish you to the greatest vigilance. Coming from below, it is of course unnecessary to warn you against any thing in the shape of decoys."

" Certainly; if we fall victims, it will be in an open fight; with our eyes open."

" Your prospect is not so gloomy, then. The Indians will not risk an open fight, and your fear must be from their treachery. We were hailed by men pretending to be in distress, but, of course, they ·were unheeded. To-night, in all probability, will be as dark as Egypt, and the red-skinned cowards will try some of their devilish games upon you. Keep together, and don't let a man sleep. If you see to-morrow morning, as I just told you, you will have to run the gauntlet. I am sorry you have a lady with you."

" It is on her account this journey is attempted. Were it otherwise, I should venture to return with you."

An hour or so slipped pleasantly by, when, with mutual good wishes, they parted company, and in a short time had lost sight of each other.

As if to give additional weight to the words of their new-made friends, the appearance of the weather changed materially. The wind, instead of blowing steadily, struck the sails in fitful gusts, and from all points of the compass, so that they were useless, and were shortly taken down. The air became colder, and whistled dismally through the forest. The sky was rapidly filled with dark clouds, that swept swiftly across the heavens, and the birds circling overhead vented their discord in shrill screams, as if frightened at the appear-ance of the elements. The river was ridged with opposing waves, and the violent wind soon filled the air with twigs and branches, that were scattered at all points over the stream.

Toward night there was a lull in the wind, and a thin, misty rain commenced falling. Shortly after, a fog concealed the banks from view, and the progress of the boats was as ʼ and as if made at night. This, although it made the situation of our friends more dismal and cheerless. was hailed by them as a fortunate occurrence. So long as they remained in the center of the river, the basilisk eyes of the Indians would fail to detect their presence. The islands which they occasionally passed were small, and they had little fear of danger from them.

Before dusk, the wind became steady, and the sails were once more hoisted. The boats being narrow, and built with an eye to speed, plowed through the water at an astonishing rate. Darkness settled slowly and heavily upon them, and they were soon wrapped in a most impenetrable gloom. They could scarcely see the length of the boat, and great care was necessary to prevent the two from parting company.

As the night progressed, the wind gradually died away, until the sails flapped, and the motion of the boats almost ceased. The oars were once more resorted to, and they again moved on, steadily but slowly, as the utmost vigilance was required to keep their position in the channel. Although most of the men were well acquainted with the windings of the Ohio, in a night of such inky blackness it could not be expected their knowledge would prove sure and certain. Several proposed to anchor and lie by until morning, but Mordaunt felt that progress was now the all-important point. They had reached the most dangerous portion of the river, where emigrants were almost sure to be troubled by enemies ; and, by working steadily all night, much might be accomplished ere morning broke. He believed their presence had not yet been discovered by the Indians, and by cautious maneuvering all would be well.

Such vague fears haunted Maude as to preclude all possibility of sleep, and, wrapping herself up to guard against the cold, drizzling fog, she took her seat at the end of the boat, to watch (if such might be the case) through the night.

"Would it not be best, Miss Maude, to secure yourself against this dismal night ?"

"I have no desire to sleep, my good friend; if I do not disturb you, I should prefer to remain here."

"You are not in our way. I only spoke for your own good. I remember that you passed but little of last night in sleep, and imagined that your body, if not your mind, demanded rest."

"I have had more than yourself, and am well able to go without sleep, when such horrors surround us ; but—"

" Lord save us! where is Mordaunt's boat?" suddenly exclaimed her companion, in amazement. All endeavored to
pierce the deep gloom, but the appalling fact forced itself
upon them that the other boat was gone! They had
unconsciously separated in the darkness!

A hurried consultation was immediately held by the men.
They believed the boats could be but a short distance
apart, and, under the circumstances, it was not prudent to
risk calling or signaling to them. Listening intently, one
or two fancied they detected the sound of oars, but the
noise was so faint the others could not be certain. The
only course to pursue was to row slowly from right to
left, and watch intently for the boat, taking great care that
the center of the stream was maintained.

This plan was acted upon at once. The men first
swerved to the right and then a long distance to the left;
they then rowed rapidly forward in the middle of the river.
They ventured to call out in suppressed tones, and purposely to splash their oars. But it availed nothing. No
answering sounds or signals were heard, and the terrible
truth was forced upon our friends. The other boat was
irretrievably gone, and the five men were now alone with
Maude Burland at the most perilous part of the journey!

It was not until this fact was certain, that the men realized their situation. A sense of utter loneliness and deso-
lation fell upon them, and they sat motionless at their
oars, undecided what to do.

" Well, it's a bad go," remarked one, in that careless
manner which a hardy spirit often evinces in danger.

" You may well say that," returned his companion; " and
how in the name of heaven we are to get out of this scrape,
I own up fair and square I can't see."

At this point one of the men, in a whisper, admonished
the last speaker to be careful in his remarks not to alarm
Maude. She overheard the caution and said:

" Don't let my presence restrain you from speaking your
thoughts. I know as well as you what our situation is, and
have lived long enough in the West not to shrink from the
name of danger."

" Miss Maude has got as brave a heart as any of us, and

for that matter, as long a head.   So what is to be said must
be heard by her, and no one knows but that *she* may see the
means to get us out of the fuss.   'Twouldn't be any thing
very strange among such a lot of thick-heads."

This good-natured sally brought a suppressed laugh to
most of the men, and served greatly to lighten their spirits.
A hopeful feeling pervaded all, at once, and Maude ventured:

" It can do us no good to remain here.   Would it not be
best to get along as far as possible under cover of this
darkness ?"

"That's the fact," responded several, dipping their oars
again.

"Howsumever," resumed the steersman, "we're going it
blind.   I'm satisfied I know as much of the Ohio, and its
twists, as any man in the boat, and I wouldn't swear we were
paddling *up* stream !"

" What ! it can not be possible we're going down the
current ?" asked one of the rowers, pausing in astonishment.

" Very possible, John.   Another thing I wouldn't swear
to; and that is that we're in *the Ohio at all.*"

" What do you mean ?" asked all, including Maude.

" Just what I said," he returned, pleasantly.   " In the
first place, it's so dark I can't see your rolling eyes this minute.   I can just make out Maude's head yonder, and the rest
of your noddles.   Every time I go to blow my nose I'm sure
to put my thumb and finger on my eyelid, and half twist it
off before I find out my mistake.   'Cause why ?   It's so dark
I can't see my own nose.   All of this goes to prove that not
one of us can swear we're in the Ohio river this minute.
We've been turning and hunting round here, and like as not
we're putting up some creek or young river."

" Whether we're going up a creek or the 'Hio, I propose
that we *go ahead.*   We'll be sure to come out *somewhere,*"
replied one of the men, with a desperate attempt at drollery.

" I don't know but that your plan is the best," resumed the
steersman.   " As long as we've *sea-room,* as we used to say in
the service, why let's stand ahead, even if we can't tell where
we're going to come out.   So dip the oars."

This was done, and the boat dashed the foam from her
brow as she cut through the resisting water.   A few moments
later and the steersman said :

"I'm rather hopeful we're on the right tack yet. Somehow or other, it *feels* as though we were in Ohio water. But if it shouldn't be so— My heavens! what's that?"

This exclamation was caused by the limb of a tree just grazing the top of his head. The next instant the boat stopped, locked in among the overhanging branches.

"Hold on! hold on!" whispered the steersman; "we've run in to shore. Just sit still until I clear the boat."

So saying, he rose in his seat, and, seizing the limbs above him, pulled the boat backward and soon extricated it.

"Now row a little slower, and I'll try and steer clear."

"Which side is this we have just touched?" asked Maude.

"The Kentucky shore," replied the steersman.

"You're mistaken," said one of the men. "It's most certainly the Ohio side."

"So it seems to me," said Maude.

"You're mistaken, both of you, and it's plain our hunt has turned all of you around. Hello! what does that mean again?" asked the steersman, ducking his head, as a mass of cold, wet leaves brushed his face.

"That cussed limb catched me right under the chin, lifted me out of my seat, and nearly sawed my head off," exclaimed the man in the front of the boat.

"Boys," said the steersman, in a changed voice, "we haven't come fifty yards since we struck the other shore. There's no use of concealing what's plain. *We're not in the Ohio, but in some infernal creek!*"

This was another startling discovery. Falling into the eddy of some stream, they had naturally pressed up it, and had not discovered their mistake until now.

"Shall we put back?" asked one, as soon as the first pause of amazement was over.

"No; it will do no good; it will only confuse us the more. I think I know the creek we're in. We'll lie here till morning, and then make up our minds what's best to do."

"Suppose we see 'sign,' what then?"

"Why, two or three of us will land, and get some idea of where we are, and we'll keep the boat close until night, when we'll pull out agin. I shouldn't wonder if Mordaunt is somewhere in the neighborhood in the same fix."

" I hope we shall find him again," said Maude, in a sorrowful voice.

"We can't till we've a little more daylight than there happens to be about just now. It can't be far from morning just now."

The night wore slowly away to the watchers. An oppressive sense of impending danger was felt by all, and for a long time the deep silence was undisturbed by a single voice.

In the course of an hour or so the darkness began to lift from the stream. Day was dawning, but it came slowly, and they saw the heavy fog still enveloped them. After a time, they could make out each others' faces, and get some idea of their situation.

" I think—"

The hand of Maude was suddenly laid upon the steersman's arm, and, gasping with terror, she pointed out in the stream. Every eye was instantly turned thither.

CHAPTER XI.

LOST! LOST!

THE men had heard the dip of oars as Maude spoke, and they now distinguished, a short distance away, the outlines of a large canoe coming down stream. Our friends hardly breathed as they came nigher and nigher. The forms of full a score of Indians could be seen sitting erect as statues, and using their paddles, Indian fashion, first on one side and then on the other. They were so close that even the ornamented scalp-locks could be made out, and the hideous war-paint and dress in which they were arrayed. Every face was turned down stream, and not the slightest deviation was made by them as they went by. It was certainly most singular that they could pass thus close to an enemy without noticing his presence.

In a moment more they had disappeared in the fog, although the sound of their paddles was still heard growing fainter and fainter, until it died out in the distance. Then one of the men ventured :

"That's the closest shave I ever seen a Shawnee or Wyandot make. Can it be possible they passed so nigh without seeing us ?"

"Not only possible, but certain," replied the steersman. "Just notice our situation, and it will not seem so curious, after all."

The men noticed now for the first time that they were concealed. The impetus of their boat had carried them far in under the overhanging branches, and through their interstices the Indian canoe had been seen. Their hiding-place was not impenetrable, but the eye of suspicion would have been the only one likely to detect them, from the canoe which had just passed.

When the day had fairly dawned, and the steersman had spent some time in looking about him, he said :

"I have been mistaken ; this is not the creek I supposed it to be. It's another one several miles above. We are further up the Ohio than I thought, which is a lucky thing, by the way. We are about two hundred yards up a creek, which puts in from Kentucky, and I suppose you can see we're upon it's right bank."

"Well, what's the plan, captain ?" asked one, addressing the steersman. "It's plain enough that Mordaunt's boat isn't likely to be seen very soon, and it's just as plain that ours is, if we venture out of here while this daylight lasts. Do you propose to wait till dark ?"

"That's the best plan, as I take it. We'll pull the boat further in, so that none going down stream will see it, and then a couple of us will step ashore and make some observations. We must find out just how we're situated."

By the aid of the limbs overhead, and by pressing the oars against the bottom of the creek, the boat was soon shoved in so far as to preclude all possibility of its being seen by any savages that might be passing down stream. This effected, the steersman and his companion, known as John, both stepped ashore, and cautiously made their way up the bank. They were both experienced woodsmen, and the most reliable men in the party. Their object, as stated above, was to reconnoiter and ascertain whether there were many Indians in the forest.

The wood surrounding them was dense and full of undergrowth; while it afforded them good cover, it necessitated the greatest care in their movements. A mis-step, or the snapping of a twig might be fatal.

They had gone but a few yards, when Hickman (the steersman) halted and snuffed the air, with a knowing look.

"Do you smell any thing?" asked his companion.

"There's a council-fire burning somewhere near us. Look yonder! Don't you see the smoke?"

A thin, bluish vapor was visible a short distance away, slowly ascending through the tree-tops. The two spies stooped, and, in a crouching position, made their way toward it. They moved slowly and stealthily, for both were sensible of the errand they were upon. After they had gone some distance further, Hickman parted the bushes in front, and the two gazed stealthily through.

Seated around a huge fire they saw twenty Indians, or more, engaged in their morning feast. They were Shawnees or Wyandots in war-costume, and most probably the company that had been seen going down the stream a few hours before.

While watching their movements, Hickman suddenly turned pale, and, fairly gasping for breath, settled back upon the ground.

"What is the matter?" asked his companion, in alarm.

"Do you not see those scalps hanging to their girdles?"

The man looked again through the bushes, and answered:

"Yes; I see several have those trophies."

"They are white men's scalps," said Hickman, his face in a gleam of excitement. "They are fresh ones. *And they are the scalps of Mordaunt's party!*"

This startling declaration of Hickman struck his companion like his own death-knell, and he sunk back with a look of mingled terror and despair.

"What's the use of trying any further? We're hemmed in by these bloodthirsty dogs, and we'll have to knock under sooner or later. I can't see the need of crawling around this way."

"Tut, tut, John, this is just the time for a man to show his mettle. Remember, we've Miss Maude in the boat."

"True, Hickman, I did not think of that. I'm willing to do what can be done, but I don't believe there is one of us that will ever see our way out again. I made up my mind to that last night when we lost the other boat."

"We're in a bad place, John, I'm free to confess, but I've been in worse. When Crawford was captured and burnt, I was followed by the Indians for over twenty miles, and I can tell you I had little time to stop and rest along the way. I tore through thickets, and creeks and streams, with the whole pack half the time in sight. I concluded it was all up with me more than once, but I come out with my hair, after all. Since then, I've made up my mind never to say die. No, no, John, there is no reason to give up yet. Remember, the Indians haven't *seen* us yet."

"But it can not be long before they will."

"That depends upon ourselves. After what we have seen, it would be our own fault if they did. That's a bad affair of the other boat—a bad affair. Let us say nothing of it to Miss Maude or the boys until we get out of the scrape."

"They'll never know it then," persisted the other.

"Let us look further—follow me, and more carefully."

The two took another direction, and an hour was spent in reconnoitering their situation. They found, as supposed, that they had run up a creek about a furlong from the Ohio. They spent a considerable time in examining the river, in hopes of finding some traces of their lost friends, but failed. Several small islands were visible in the stream, and in between a couple of these Hickman fancied he saw a signal. He climbed a tree, and carefully scrutinized it, but failed to satisfy himself of its nature. A species of low shrubbery that covered the island prevented him from ascertaining whether it was an Indian canoe or the boat of their lost friends which supported the suspicious object. It appeared as if a man in a stooping position was holding his rifle-barrel over his head, from the muzzle of which a rag or handkerchief was fluttering.

"That means something, and I believe that rag is held by a white man, John. What do you make of it?"

His companion had ascended, and was seated on a limb beside him.

"It beats my time, but I'm afraid it's a decoy. If Colonel Mordaunt were living, he would not be in such a place as that, and who else could it be who would seek to befriend us?"

"I was on a scout with Dick Dingle once, and we got into good deal of such a muss as this—that is, he and I had to separate for a while, and the way I found him again was by just such a contrivance as that. He stuck a rag up on his gun-barrel, when forty redskins stood as good chance of seeing it as I did. It did what he wanted it to for all that."

"But Dick Dingle can not be there."

"It don't seem possible, and yet I thought of him the minute my eye caught that."

Our two friends hardly removed their eyes from the signal for a long time, in the hope that something more satisfactory would soon be detected. It remained perfectly stationary for perhaps twenty minutes, when it disappeared altogether. As it was lowered, an instant flash in the sunlight proved that it had indeed been supported by a rifle-barrel.

"There is *some one* who knows we're here," said Hickman, "and I would give a year from my life if it would tell me who is among those islands. But we must return, or there will be fears on account of our absence."

On the ground our friends paused again and gazed toward the islands mentioned; but they saw nothing more; and, deeply perplexed at the turn matters had taken, they made their way back to the boat. It required considerable labor to discover their friends, so carefully had their concealment been made. When they did, as may be supposed, they were in considerable trepidation. Hickman stated that a large party of Indians were encamped above them, but as yet they knew nothing of their own proximity.

"And did you learn nothing of father?" asked Maude, turning an appealing look toward him.

The question was so direct and unexpected that Hickman coughed and showed some hesitation before he replied:

"We have not seen them, Miss Maude; but we saw something else which I think may encourage us to hope."

"What was that?" she asked, so breathlessly that Hickman's heart chided him at the hopes his remark had given her.

"It was nothing regarding Mr. Mordaunt. I think you should be rejoiced that we have not seen him in this neighborhood. Out among the islands we discovered something which we believe is proof that we have *friends*, at least, as well as enemies at hand."

Hickman thereupon related what is already known to the reader. He was disappointed, however, in the effect produced by the information. It produced only speculation and doubt, and one or two freely expressed their opinion that it was some decoy of their enemies.

It was decided to remain in their present concealment until night, when they could drop down into the river and venture once more upon their journey. The fog having been dissipated by the rising sun, it was only by the greatest care and the best of fortune that they could hope to elude the treacherous savages.

Nothing occurred to excite new alarm with our friends until late in the afternoon. It was then that the breaking of twigs was heard above them upon the bank, as though persons were passing to and fro. Hickman raised his hand to enjoin perfect silence, and bent his head and listened. The sounds were heard once or twice more, when they ceased. He waited several minutes, when, to dissipate the terror that had seized several of his companions, he said:

"'Tis a good omen; such carelessness proves that they suspect nothing."

"Will they not notice the trail we made?"

"I trust not, as they have no reason to believe that strangers are in the wood."

At that instant a dark, ball-like body dropped lightly from the tree which sheltered them, and whisked off in the darkness.

"What was that?" asked Hickman. "Did any one see it?"

"I did," replied Maude. "It was an Indian; I saw his black eyes gleaming among the leaves the instant before he dropped to the ground."

"Quick! your oars then! We are discovered! There's not a second to lose!"

The men did as commanded, and two others rose to assist them by using the branches around them. With a yell they sprung overboard, and endeavored to make their way to land.

"For God's sake, exert yourselves !" cried Hickman, seizing an oar himself. "Into the cabin, Miss Maude, quick, I command you !"

Hardly knowing what she did, Maude hurriedly obeyed this command. She felt the boat moving, and a minute after it rocked fearfully, and the sound of scuffling feet was heard overhead. Wishing to shut out the dreadful sounds, she stopped her ears, and bent her head in agonizing prayer. Still the reports of the rifles, the shouts of rage, and yells of death were only muffled, and her soul took in the awful scene that was going on above her.

She was not in a situation to judge of the lapse of time. She seemed to live an age in those brief seconds. She did not notice the cessation of the direful noises—not until she heard the words :

"You come up here. You will not be harmed."

Not until she heard these words, we say, did she look up. As she turned her gaze toward the speaker, she saw the face of *Monowano* peering down upon her. This additional shock nearly deprived her of reason for the instant ; but, bracing her heart, she arose and made her way toward him. He reached and took her hand, and hurriedly whispered :

"Monowano tried to save your friends, but could not. He will save you or die for you. Don't show that you know me."

She made no reply, for, by the time she comprehended his words, she was in the midst of a band of reeking, exultant savages. As she gazed about her, a suspicion that Monowano was deceiving her filled her with sickening terror. Around her were the repelling evidences of the desperate conflict that had just terminated. Several fresh scalps were suspended at the girdles of the savages, but not a white man was visible. All, she believed, had fallen.

There were about a dozen Indians, whose scowling visages were turned toward her as she made her appearance. They halted but a moment, however ; the boat was fast against the bank, and, springing ashore, assisted by Monowano, she was led away into the wilderness.

CHAPTER XII

AN APPARITION AND A VISITATION.

MAUDE was led to the fire of the savages, where Hickman and his companion had first discovered them. Here they halted and held a long consultation; others joined them from the wood, until there were about twenty. As hinted before, they were upon the war-path, and the debate was upon the disposal of the prisoner. At that time it was very common for the Indians to retain their female prisoners as captives, and to slay the men.

The savages in question were in this neighborhood for the purpose of intercepting flat-boats going down the river, and it was a long way to their nearest town. They deemed it nardly necessary for the whole force to take the captive in charge, and thus perhaps lose several golden opportunities for plunder and murder. Accordingly, it was determined to dispatch five of their number with Maude to one of their towns, where her fate should be determined. The rest were to remain and continue their present outrages as chance offered.

As fortune would have it, Monowano was appointed one of the five. The decision of the savages was acted upon at once. The greater number filed off in the woods and disappeared; and, shortly after, Monowano, followed by his four dusky companions, with Maude between them, plunged into the forest.

A mile or two ahead, it became necessary to cross a river. After much difficulty, Monowano found a canoe in which Maude was placed and carried safely across. During the proceeding the mysterious Indian found occasion to say:

"Keep a good heart. To-morrow's sun shall see you free or never rise upon Monowano."

These words and the subsequent actions of the Indians had little effect upon Maude. The scenes of terror through which she had passed produced a sort of stupor and indifference to her fate. When told to walk or halt, she did so, mechanically, and without question or murmur. Monowano noticed the vacant, meaningless expression of her face, and strove to attract her attention and create an interest in their movements. Now and then she drew a deep breath as if some heavy weight oppressed her; but as yet she had not even shown that she comprehended the words that had been said to her.

The march through the forest was very deliberate and easy; and ere half the afternoon had elapsed, a halt was made. A fire was kindled and some *hominy* cooked. Monowano brought some of this to where Maude was seated on the ground, and, kneeling as he handed it to her, said:

"We have stopped for the night. Keep your eyes open and see every thing!"

For the first time Maude seemed to awaken to a sense of her situation. Monowano saw it by the sudden gleam in her eyes. He said no more and did not pause longer by her, for he wished to attach no suspicion to his conduct.

Maude accepted the proffered food and ate a small portion. Then she betook herself to watching the movements of the Indians with the most painful interest. She was seated by herself. No offer had been made to bind her, as such a precaution was unnecessary. After a while, however, one of the Indians came toward her, and, holding a thong made of deer-skin, motioned for her to rise. She did so, when he led her to a small tree and proceeded to bind her. He had passed the thong around her waist, and was in the act of fastening it to the tree, when he was seized and flung a dozen feet with great violence. As the discomfited savage arose, he saw the indignant Monowano standing before him, his face livid with furious passion. His dark eyes seemed to dart fire upon him, and his chest heaved like the waves of the sea. Suddenly Maude whispered. He was standing between her and the fallen savage, and his face was from her. As he caught the sound of her voice, he did not change his position or the dreadful expression of his countenance, but Maude knew he was listening with his whole soul to catch her words.

"Bind me, Monowano. It will not give me pain, and it will be best for both of us."

As the crestfallen Indian joined his companions, Monowano, with the dignity of a king, turned and picked up the thong which had fallen at Maude's feet. With the greatest care he wound it around her body and secured it to the sapling.

"Does it hurt you?" he asked, as he had finished.

"Not in the least; have no fears on that account."

He then left her, and approached the fire. Lighting his pipe, he seated himself a few feet from the blaze, then, folding his blanket around him, he disdained to hold conversation with the other four. The latter were occupied in the same manner with the most stoical indifference, and it was evident that if no interruption occurred, they would remain thus for several hours.

Maude was about a dozen yards distant. She was bound so loosely that she felt she could free herself the minute she chose. She gazed at the smoking savages a few minutes and then allowed her eyes to wander in another direction. It was with that absent expression which is seen when the mind is intently occupied, that her gaze roved over the forest.

Fixed upon no particular point or object, her heart suddenly throbbed as her eyes were turned upon a spot about a hundred yards distant.

She saw a knot-like protuberance slowly rise from behind a fallen tree, until the coon-skin cap of a hunter was visible, and finally two eyes could be seen glaring among a mass of shaggy locks. So distinctly was the startling sight imprinted upon her vision, that she detected the nervous, restless tremor of the eye, so peculiar to the frontier character. The head remained in full view for the space of a minute, when it dropped out of sight.

Almost immediately, at the opposite end of the log, another exhibition, somewhat similar, took place. The head, instead of coming up slowly and cautiously bobbed to the right and left, as if its owner were timid about exposing his person, and then all at once shot upward so much that not only the head but the shoulders of a man were seen for the instant. It was with strange emotion that Maude recognized the head as belonging to Pete Jenkins!

Her first feeling was that of joy, and the knowledge that friends were so near. Not until she recalled the circumstances

under which they had parted company with him, did this feeling change to alarm. His threats had not been forgotten, and
she reflected that her fate might become infinitely worse than
it already was. The appearance of his companion filled her
with additional terror. At first thought it occurred that he
might be one of the members of their party; but, as she
recalled their faces one by one, she found none which could
correspond with the glowing eyes and shaggy, exuberant
hair. He was a stranger, at least, and probably some desperate
white savage, that Jenkins had picked up and joined with
him for the purpose of revenging himself for the treatment he
had received.

As she again raised her eyes toward the tree, a rifle-barrel
was projected about a foot above it, and from the muzzle—
fluttered a handkerchief—the same signal that had so puzzled
Hickman and his companion. Maude was more at a loss to
understand what this meant than any thing she had witnessed
thus far. The signal was lowered in a moment, and then the
shaggy, repulsive face made its appearance. Ere this disappeared, Maude reflected that the object of these different
stratagems might be to attract her attention, and whoever
were concealed behind the log were waiting for some evidence
that such was the case.

Glancing toward the Indians, she saw one of them was
replenishing the fire and the others lazily watching him.
Quick as thought she raised her hand, and, accompanying it
with a motion of the head, gave the sign. The shaggy
object seemed satisfied, and again made itself invisible.

During the next hour her eyes hardly left the tree, but
she detected nothing that might show her there were other
human beings than her captors in the neighborhood. It
soon became so dark that the outlines of the log were barely
discernible, and at length blended with the darkness.

Maude began to experience the inconveniences of her situation. Although the ligature scarcely confined her arms, she
felt cramped and pained from maintaining one position. So,
to better matters, she quietly freed her arms and folded them
before her. She saw the eyes of Monowano were constantly
wandering toward her, as though he was revolving some
scheme in his mind, and the looks of the others scarcely

left her; yet the gloom was so great she believed they would not notice this circumstance. She bore her trials bravely, for she was nerved by hope. She confidently believed Mono-wano would prove as good as his promise; and, although the loss of her companions was a blow from which it seemed she could never recover, yet the hope of life within her own bosom was strong enough to keep her spirits from sinking to that despair which she before had felt.

The relief felt from freeing her hands was so comforting, that she proceeded further—quietly drawing her feet through the lax thongs, and actually liberating her entire body. As she glanced toward her captors, she saw their suspicion was roused by her movements. One of them, with an impatient "ugh," arose and walked toward her. When within a dozen feet, he sprung high in the air with a sharp yell of agony, and rolled over on the ground in the pains of death.

The others, seeing they were attacked, grasped their weapons and sprung to their feet. At the same instant the sharp, whip-like crack of another rifle was heard, and a second Indian bit the dust. There were now two Indians, besides Monowano. The latter, at the first alarm, grasped his toma-hawk, and stood glaring around him like an animal at bay. One of the others dashed off in the forest, and the remaining one, with a shout of fury, drew his knife and rushed toward Maude, intending to defeat her rescuers at the last moment. His purpose could have hardly been divined, before some-thing was seen to flash for a second over the head of Mono-wano, and the next his gleaming tomahawk shot like a meteor from his upraised arm, and the savage fell to the ground, his skull cloven in twain.

The next moment Dick Dingle and Pete Jenkins rushed into the clearing.

"Lord bless you, Maude! Are you hurt?" asked the latter, running toward her.

"Thank Heaven! no," she answered, falling forward and fainting in his arms.

"Oh blazes! ain't this nice!" said he, as he braced himself in the expectation of sustaining her entire weight. "I'll tend to her, Monowano. You needn't come here, Dingle, she's all right."

"Just wait till I do some ha'r raisin'," replied the old

hunter. Whereupon he proceeded to scalp the unconscious Indians that lay around him. While this was going on, Mono-wano stood as motionless as a statue. His eyes followed the motions of Dingle as he went through his revolting opera-tions, and then turned toward Maude as she recovered her senses.

"Are you two the only ones?" she asked, with a bewil-dered look.

"We are the only ones; but it's plain we was enough," returned Jenkins, pompously. "How do you feel, my dear?"

"I feel better," she replied, relieving herself from his sup-port. At this moment Dingle approached.

"We've got a long road to travel, and don't you think we'd better be about it, Monowano?"

"The path is long, and the eyes of the Shawnee are upon it," replied the Indian, approaching Maude, and speaking for the first time.

"Let's be off, then."

CHAPTER XIII

THE STORY OF THE SIGNAL.

WHEN Jenkins was left upon shore, during the night, by the party whose safety he had so much endangered, he was fully impressed with the danger of his situation. Accord-ingly, after he had given vent to the third cry of "Murder!" and opened his eyes and found that he was indeed alone, he concluded his own safety demanded a different course. He stood upon the margin of a vast wilderness, with no idea of his situation further than that he was somewhere in the "Dark and Bloody Ground," and liable at any moment to encounter his deadliest enemies.

He waited awhile in the hopes of discerning the boats of his relenting friends, but was disappointed; and, fearful that his outcry might have attracted the attention of other than friends, he made his way further into the woods. Being completely lost, he lay down, and, pulling the leaves over him, went to sleep.

He was in the midst of a fearful dream of Indians, when he was aroused by a severe kick. Looking up, he was greatly amazed and gratified to see Dick Dingle standing near him.

"How comes this? Off on an adventure of yer own? What's 'come of the boats?"

"They put me on shore, Dick, and left me," said he, with a rueful countenance, as he arose to his feet.

"What fur?"

"'Cause I talked too much. Dern 'em, they kept talking all the time."

"You made too much noise, eh?"

"So they said."

"Didn't they tell you beforehand to stop?"

"No—yes; they kind of told me six or seven times; but it was a mean trick."

"Sarved you right," bluntly replied the hunter.

"They'll suffer for it," said Jenkins, shaking his head. "I told 'em what they might expect."

"What was that?"

"Death and torture at the stake."

"How you goin' to do that ar' thing?"

"Why, stir up the Injins; that's how! I'll tell Sime Girty how they served me, and we'll head an expedition against 'em."

A low, taunting laugh issued from Dingle's mouth, as he leaned against a tree and gave vent to his mirth.

"What you laughing at?" indignantly demanded Jenkins.

"Stir up Injins—tell Sime Girty—head an expedition—oh! that's a *leetle too much* for Dick Dingle."

And thereupon the ranger let his back slide down the tree, and, dropping limberly to the ground, indulged freely in his silent merriment. Jenkins' threats had been uttered in earnest, both to Mordaunt and to Dingle, but the ridicule of the latter made him repent them most heartily.

"I was only in fun, Dingle," said he; "I just wanted to fool you. Get up, and don't make such a dunce of yourself. How come you to find me?"

Dingle's excessive jollity immediately ended, and he arose and said:

"I heard some one hollerin' '*murder*,' last night. Any idea who 'twas ?"

"It was me," returned Jenkins, rather sheepishly. "I wanted to scare them in the boat."

"I heard, as I's sayin', and knowed 'twas you, and s'pected the heathen had got you. So I thought it wouldn't do to come very nigh you, or let you know I was about, till I could see how things stood. Consequently, I waited till daylight, and then come down on you."

"How come you to be in these parts, I mean ?"

"I was comin' up from below," replied Dingle, with a sober air.

"What's the news ?"

"Bad—bad," replied the ranger, shaking his head slowly. from side to side, and gazing thoughtfully at the ground.

"The Shawnees at their tricks again ?"

"Not the Shawnees alone, but the Delawares, Wyandots, Mingoes and Miamis are at it, and it's my opine it was the luckiest stroke of your life when you was dumped on shore. Those two boats will never see Pittsburg !"

Jenkins' eyes opened with horror, and, in place of the spite and rage he entertained just now for the party, was the most earnest commiseration for them. He felt brave enough to do any thing to avert the blow that seemed impending over them.

"Can't one do any thing to help them ?" he asked.

"We can try."

Whereupon Dingle instantly turned and plunged into the forest, going in a direction that led up the river. So rapid were his footsteps, that Jenkins was compelled to jump over bushes, stumble over roots and briers, and maintain a sort of compromise between a walk and run, to prevent falling behind.

It is not our purpose to weary the reader with a detailed account of the manner in which these two characters discovered the whereabouts of their friends. The wonderful skill of Dingle proved equal to the task. When the boat whose fortunes we have followed put into the creek, he and Jenkins were upon shore, and plainly heard the noise of their paddles, slight as it was. More than once the ranger was on the point of calling out to them, but his habitual prudence prevailed. He endeavored to follow it, but the nature of the ground prevented, and when our friends put in to shore, he lost all track of them.

He more than half suspected the darkness had separated the boats, and, believing one would cruise around in the river in search of the other, he and Jenkins swam over to several islands which lay near the center of the stream. By taking this course, he knew no boat could pass him without his knowledge; while, had he remained on shore, such a thing could have easily occurred. On these islands the two trail-hunters passed the entire night, without learning any thing more regarding their friends. Jenkins, however, detected the glimmer of a fire through the leaves, and Dingle swam over to the mainland, and reconnoitered it. As the reader has probably suspected, this was the camp-fire of the Indians, seen by Hickman and his companion.

Ascertaining this much, Dingle rejoined Jenkins upon the islands, and waited for daylight before attempting any thing further. The large canoe, full of savages, was seen by them as it emerged from the creek, and almost satisfied them that it was the one which they had mistaken for their friends. But a lingering suspicion that the case was different, induced them to remain in their present position.

Knowing further that when the whites discovered the error they had committed, they would send out some of their number to determine their locality, Dingle fixed upon some means of attracting their attention. He would have recrossed to the mainland, had he not been certain the river was watched by more than one pair of lynx eyes, and his movement would have been assuredly seen. Believing the scouts of their friends would not fail to scrutinize the islands, he adopted the artifice mentioned—that of placing a piece of his hunting-shirt upon the end of his rifle; and, while holding it over his head, he and Jenkins were lying flat upon their faces sweeping the shore with eagle eyes, to ascertain whether it had attracted notice.

Had this signal been seen by Mordaunt, it would have been understood at once, as he and Dingle had used the same before; but, of course, Mordaunt saw nothing of it; and it has been shown that, although observed by Hickman and his friend, they failed to comprehend its significance.

Shortly after the conflict took place, Dingle, regardless of consequences, plunged into the stream and struck out for the land. Jenkins followed, and, when near the shore, cried out that he was taken with the cramp. Dingle replied that he would come back toward night and help him, if he had not recovered by that time, and kept on—Jenkins, despite his cramp, landing nearly at the same instant.

But, even before this, the sounds of death had ceased, and a vapory mass of smoke that came filtering through the tree-tops was all that showed where the awful scene had taken place. A careful reconnoitering disclosed to Dingle the true state of affairs. He saw the Indians separate, and Maude given to the care of Monowano. This fact satisfied him that the Indian, about whom there was so much speculation and mystery, was one of the most dangerous foes to the whites. Dingle, although grateful for the services shown him by this Indian, believed they had only been a ruse to conceal his true intentions. That he had been the main instrument in the destruction of the boats, he was satisfied, and, as a reward, the maiden he had so long sought had been given to him by the others.

Dingle formed his determination, but communicated neither that nor his suspicions to Jenkins. When he saw how weak the party was, he proposed to his companion to follow it and attempt a rescue. The latter could not refuse, although he manifested some reluctance, and they dogged the savages' footsteps until they halted, when they maneuvered around them until Maude's attention was attracted. The subsequent events have already been given.

CHAPTER XIV

IN THE WOODS, AND ITS TRAGEDY.

DINGLE's resolution was that Monowano should return with him to the settlement, where he should receive the punishment decided upon by the settlers themselves. If the Indian refused to accompany him, he resolved to shoot him on the spot, and bear his scalp in as a trophy. To his surprise, however, he volunteered to go with him, and to facilitate matters the trail-hunter kept up every appearance of friendship and confidence.

As the homeward journey compelled them to travel on foot the entire distance, it of course required considerable time and care. Maude was weakened by the scenes through which she had passed, and their progress was accommodated to her disposition. Dingle, from his intimate knowledge of the country, took the lead. Jenkins and Maude followed at a distance of a few yards, while Monowano strode silently in the rear.

Jenkins was in exuberant spirits, and Dingle, knowing it was impossible to restrain his tongue, allowed him to rattle on without interruption :

" Must have felt scar't considerably much, Maude ?" said he, looking around inquiringly in her face.

" Yes, we were all sorely alarmed when we found that the boats had separated in the darkness."

" That was rather odd. 'Twouldn't happened if I'd been on board. Mordaunt couldn't have slipped off without my seeing him. Ah, well !" said Jenkins, heaving a great sigh, " I s'pose it was a retribution visited upon them by Providence for serving me as they did."

" Was it not for your own good ?" asked Maude, in a reproving tone.

" Well, so it seems. I don't know though, after all. If I'd

been with you, you would have hardly made such a mistake as to run into that creek supposing it to be the Ohio."

"We had lost completely our situation from rowing around in search of my dear father's boat."

"I know—I know there's some excuse for the mistake, but even after committing it, you ought to have repelled them Injins. If I'd been with you, now, you might have stood a chance—"

Jenkins paused as he saw Dingle had overheard him, and was looking around with one of his droll, sarcastic looks.

"Are you tired, dear?" he asked, affectionately.

"No; I can walk for hours yet. Are you not fatigued?"

"Me? gracious alive. I never get tired. I wonder how Monowano feels."

Jenkins and Maude both turned to look at the Indian. He was walking thoughtfully along, his head bent, so that he failed to see their looks. They said nothing to him, but resumed their conversation.

"If I were sure my dear father had escaped these ruthless savages, I would ask no greater mercy. It is strange, the manner in which he was lost."

"Oh! I guess he's all right!" said Jenkins, elevating his eyebrows as though there could be no doubt about his safety.

"Have you any just reason for thinking so?"

"Have you any reason for thinking differently?"

"I have none but what my own fears bring up. His situation was such that it seems impossible for him to have escaped."

"It was rather bad, I allow. You asked me just now whether I had any reason for believing he had given the Injins the slip, and I believe I have. In the first place, had they been attacked, the sounds of their guns and the unearthly screeching of the imps would have been heard by you, as they couldn't have been a very great ways off. I shouldn't wonder if they put in to shore, and took the land for Pittsburg, or to some place further up the river, where the Injins wasn't so thick. Howsumever, if they've been rubbed out of existence, Monowano here behind us would be likely to know something about it. I'll just ask him. Say, you, Monowano."

The Indian raised his head and waited for his question.

"Do you know any thing of Mordaunt and his party? Maude here, or the Evening Star, as you call her, would like to know whether they're in the land of the living or not."

"Monowano knows nothing of them," replied the Indian, dropping his head and resuming his thoughtful mien, as if to repel further inquiry.

"That settles the matter," said Jenkins, triumphantly. "There couldn't have been any fighting going on within a dozen miles of that chap without his knowing. He's rather cute considering his skin is red."

"Father may have escaped, then," said Maude, as if communing with herself, and without heeding the last remark of Jenkins. "He may have gone overland as you said; but how will he ever reach Pittsburg, and how shall I ever see him again?"

"Don't trouble yourself about that, dear Maude," said Jenkins, rather affectionately. "After a time I'll go up to Pittsburg and tell him about it, and bring him back, or take you to him if you should prefer it. Ah! here's quite a little stream to be crossed."

They had reached a brook some six or eight feet wide, across which Jenkins manifested great anxiety to assist his charge. There was no real difficulty, however, presented, as several stones afforded places for the feet.

"Hadn't I better take you in my arms and carry you across?" he asked.

"There is no need of that," she replied, smiling at his readiness.

"Oh! yes, I think you had better let me do it."

Before she suspected his intention, he lifted her in his arms and stepped out in the stream. As he held her before him, he could not very well see where to place his feet, and the consequence was that just half way across, he fell flat upon his back. Fearful for his own safety, he instantly relinquished her and scrambled around to save himself. When the mishap occurred, Monowano sprung forward as quick as thought and landed Maude safe and dry upon the bank before she was hardly aware Jenkins had made such a mis-step.

The latter came panting to the shore, somewhat discomfited by the accident.

"Did you get one of your faintin' fits that time, Jenkins?" asked Dingle.

"None of your business! You just go on ahead, and I'll tend to her. I don't s'pose you ever had a fall. I'll tend to Maude, if you please, Monowano."

The Indian fell behind at once without a word, and the journey was continued as though it had suffered no interruption. Jenkins had just decided upon a sentence to recommence the conversation, when Dingle raised his hand above his head and gave utterance to a sudden

"Whisht!"

Those in the rear halted, and saw the trail-hunter sink to the earth as though examining something on the ground. In an instant he arose, and motioned for the Indian to come to his side. The latter did so, and they carefully scrutinized the ground.

"What do you make of it?" asked Dingle.

"'Tis the blood of a white man who is nigh at hand."

"My idee exactly. S'posen we beat around, Monowano?"

This was acted upon at once, but for a time without success. The trail, after several singular turnings, led back to the brook, where it disappeared in the water.

"Some poor feller has tried to give the heathen a slip by taking to the water," muttered Dingle. Poor chap! if he's been winged, as I allow it's pretty plain from the look of things in these parts, he's had some trouble."

At this instant, Dingle started as he plainly heard the groan of a human being. He listened for its repetition and called out:

"Whoever you be, sing out; there's nobody in these parts that'll harm ye."

"Is that Dick Dingle?" asked a voice directly behind him.

The hunter wheeled and saw, peering through the bushes at him with a wondering, agonizing expression, the face of Hickman, the steersman.

"I reckon it is. How is it with you? Hurt much?"

"I'm afraid, Dick, I have got my last wound. Who have you got with you?"

"Miss Maude, Jenkins and Monowano."

"You've got the girl away from them have you? I'm glad

to hear it. Well, Dingle, there's no use of trying to hide it, I've got about twenty minutes to stay above ground, and if you will do me the favor to stand by me till the sickness is over, you will do me a kindness that I will remember as long as I live," he said, with a ghastly smile. "Just tell Jenkins and the others to keep back out of sight, will you? I would rather not have any one near but you."

The trail-hunter hastened to Monowano and Jenkins, and told them he had come across a friend who was dying and who wished to be left alone with himself. The three withdrew further into the wood, where they promised to await his return.

"It's clever in you, Dick," said the dying man, as he came back.

"Don't say any thing about it—don't say any thing about it, Hickman. I expect I'll want some one to stand by when I go under, and the man who won't do that turn for another is worse than a Shawnee. How was it you got this hurt, Hickman?"

"I was on the boat, when they came down upon us. As soon as I saw it was all up with us, I made a jump and a run for it. One of them followed me almost all the way here, when I stopped and had a death hug with him. I finished him and he finished me."

"This Monowano—what part did he play in the scrimmage?"

"It's hard to tell, Dick; I don't know what to think of him. I did not see him strike a blow, and yet I believe he must be one of the ringleaders. He must have helped the destruction of Mordaunt's party."

"Freeze me to death! have they gone under, too?" asked Dingle, with a recoil of amazement.

"That's my opinion, and although it's as certain as a thing can well be, yet I couldn't swear to it. They had half a dozen white scalps besides our party's, and as they looked fresh, it seems to me they couldn't have well been any one else's besides Mordaunt's and his men."

"It must be them, though it's strange, I allow, that I didn't hear any thing of it when it happened."

"They must have stolen on them and attacked them before

they had any chance to prepare for it. It's a bad blow for Miss Maude, Dick, and I wouldn't say any thing of it for a while. Whew! my wind is bad."

" Where is it, Hickman ?"

" Right in my side here is the spot where his knife entered. There's no use of fussing with it. I bandaged it up so that it will last as long as it's intended. Just ease me down a little, Dick, on my left side."

Dingle carefully placed the man more at ease, and asked:

" Is there any thing you'll want done—any word you'd like to send to the settlement ?"

" My brother is there—we two were orphans and without any other relation living. Just give him the particulars of my accident—tell him how we did all we could—"

" There's no need of tellin' any one that," interrupted Dingle, with a feeling that was of great credit to him. " We all know that, Hickman, and so just save yourself of tellin' what ain't no use."

" Well, give him the particulars then, Dick, and tell them your own story. And give my dying love to him. I know of nothing else to send ; but about that Monowano, Dick, do you know what my idea is ?"

" What is it ?"

" I believe he's a white man or a half-breed, and a renegade in disguise. He saved your life once, I know ; but I believe he has sent more out the world than he ever prevented from going."

" That's purty much my idee, and he'll be overhauled when he gets back to the settlement. This has been a job rather too big for him to undertake. He's been asked several times bout himself, but hain't never give anybody satisfaction, and ve've been fools enough to let him pull the wool over our eyes ; but he won't do it longer."

" I'd like to live long enough to find out who and what he is, but that can't be. The first thing you do after you get him in limbo, try that paint on him. See whether water and scrubbing will change its color. You know how long Jim Peterson's wife was believed to be an Indian. He met her dozens of times in the woods, without ever once dreaming that she was a white girl and had promised to be his wife. There may be something like this with this Indian."

"It'll be all cleared up when we get back there. Couldn't you manage to get up enough gumption to walk there and wait till the thing is done with, before you go under?" asked the trail-hunter, with a burst of hopefulness.

"Ah, no, Dick!" replied Hickman, with a wan, sickly smile; "it's a wonder that I have held up thus long. I have bled terribly, as you must have seen."

"Yes, yes; it's no mistake to say you got a bad stick—a bad stick, Hickman. How do you feel now?"

"I've managed to stop this flow of blood, and that seems to have held in my breath; but it can't last much longer. I wouldn't tell Miss Maude—I guess—"

"What do you say?"

"It wouldn't be right—it might alarm her. Boys, be careful, and don't make a noise, for the Indians are around us—"

Dingle saw that his mind was wandering, and with much care lifted him nearer an upright position. The poor fellow still pressed the bandages to his wound; and, as they seemed to have dried to their place, not a drop of his life-blood escaped. As his head was raised, he slowly opened his eyes and gazed languidly about him with that vacant, dreamy and unsettled expression often seen in deep revery. Several times his eyes passed over the trail-hunter's face without noting it; but after an effort to look behind him, as if in fear, they gradually settled upon his countenance. Here they rested fully a minute, their light gradually increasing and becoming more intelligent, until a slight smile played around his mouth, and his lips opened:

"I've been light-headed, haven't I, Dick?"

"You was a little."

"What did I say?"

"Nothin', only something about not telling Maude."

"Nothing else?" asked Hickman, discovering a singular interest.

"You 'peared to think you was in the boat talkin' to the boys; that's all you said, I believe."

"Ah! I remember now a sort of dream—but, Dingle, am I not trespassing upon your forbearance?"

It seems strange that such an idea as this is almost sure to present itself to the man stricken down by sudden sickness, and that, apparently, his greatest anxiety is upon the same ground.

"Freeze me! Hickman, don't say nothin' 'bout that agin. It don't sound like a man. But I s'pose you have made up your mind to go under, and what's your wish about your body?"

"Are you willing to dig me a grave? It will be severe work."

"The ground is soft here, and Monowano's tomahawk, my knife, and our hands will soon do it. Don't think of that."

"Well, then, dig it here—right on the spot where I lie. You will have to cover it up nicely, for if they get on the trail, they will follow it for the scalp."

"Trust us for that."

"I have nothing else—remember not to tell Miss Maude—my brother—Lord, have mercy on me—"

All expression retreated suddenly from the eyes, and Hickman dropped over perfectly lifeless.

Dingle waited a moment for signs of life; but finding he was indeed dead, he straightened his limbs out. In doing so, he detected several other wounds of which the man had said nothing. It was evident he had been engaged in a most deadly hand-to-hand conflict, and had struggled manfully for life. His garments were torn and lacerated, as if clutched and cut by the knife, and the wonder to the trail-hunter was that he had survived as long as he did.

He signaled to Jenkins and Monowano to approach. As they came up, he briefly related the particulars of his death, saying nothing, however, of the fate of Mordaunt's party, and stated his wishes about his burial. The three set to work at once, Dingle with his knife and the Indian with his tomahawk. As the ground was loosened, Jenkins threw it out with his naked hands, and the work progressed much more rapidly than would have been supposed.

In this manner they wrought for a couple of hours, when the grave was of sufficient depth. The dead body was then lowered into it, and carefully covered. The sod, which had been cut and removed with the greatest care, was replaced with remarkable nicety, and all traces of the fresh earth concealed. To guard still more effectually against discovery,

Dingle cut off several bushes and stuck them in the ground directly over the grave. This was done with so much art that none but the most experienced eye would have detected the cheat.

All that could be done for the dead man was now done, and our friends once more turned their faces homeward. The feelings of the whites were saddened by what they had witnessed, and the journey was maintained in the most gloomy silence. They felt that the fate of Hickman was liable to be their own at any minute. The very forest through which they were proceeding was swarming with hordes of Indians, who would follow their trail with the persistency of the bloodhound.

No halt was made until the gathering darkness in the woods admonished them the sun had set and night was nigh at hand. Then they "camped" in a sort of hollow or valley-like depression, and prepared to spend the night.

CHAPTER XV

CONCLUSION.

DINGLE maintained watch through the night, which passed away without any thing occurring to alarm the party. Several birds had been brought down the day before by his rifle, so that nothing was wanted by the party in the way of food.

At the first appearance of day, the little party was astir. Their meal was partaken of in silence, and the march resumed in the same manner as upon the preceding day. Monowano seemed more thoughtful than ever, and barely replied to the direct questions put to him. Dingle manifested a cheerfulness and a confidence in him that he was far from feeling. Under the pretense of watching the movements of Jenkins, he kept the Indian continually under his eye, although from his actions he was satisfied he would make no attempt to flee.

To guard against danger from every point, Jenkins was sent on the back trail, Dingle instructing him to proceed a

8

half-mile or so with his *usual care*. As soon as he had disappeared upon this duty, Dingle walked slowly onward, closely followed by Maude and Monowano, all listening for any signal from Jenkins. In this manner they had progressed but a few yards, when they were startled by the most heart-rending cries of:

"Murder!—Injins!—Injins!—Shawnees!—Delawares!—Wyandots!—Tecumseh!—Sime Girty!—Murder!—Help! help!"

As quick as thought, Dingle threw his right arm around Maude and darted several yards to the left, where he ordered her to seat herself upon the ground while he stationed himself behind a large tree, where, with rifle ready-cocked, he waited the assault of his enemies. Monowano had disappeared, and a thought of treachery flashed across the mind of the trail-hunter as he peered cautiously out from his concealment. He only compressed his lips the tighter, and muttered:

"Freeze me! ef it's so, it's the last time; fur ef I don't make daylight shine through that skull of his, it'll be because Dick Dingle has forgot to pull a trigger."

A terrific crashing and snapping of the bushes was now heard, and the next instant Jenkins burst into view, his hat gone, his hair flying, and his eyes fairly bursting with terror. He was running with desperate speed, and about ten feet behind him a monstrous black bear was leisurely cantering, apparently indulging in the race not for his prey but merely out of pure mischief. The brute had hardly appeared before the short, explosive crack of Monowano's rifle was heard, and he tumbled headlong on the ground, Jenkins falling at the same instant, and shouting:

"I'm killed! I'm killed! Dingle, come bury me!"

As the laughing trail-hunter stepped from his concealment, he saw Monowano plunging his knife to the hilt in the body of the bear, which shortly gasped out its life. He approached without paying the least attention to the rolling, kicking, shouting Jenkins. The latter continued his struggles and cries a moment longer, when he suddenly stopped, lifted up his head and looked around him. Then he clapped his hand to his head, rubbed his poll, and examined his hand to see whether there was blood upon it. Seeing none, he twisted his arm 'over his back and rubbed it around there awhile. At this point, had Dingle listened, he might have heard him say to himself:

" I wonder whether I was shot or not. Derned if I believe I was. Yender's Dick and the Injin, too ! I'd like to know whether they noticed me !"

Dingle and Monowano had just turned to join Maude, who had not stirred from the situation in which she had been placed, when Jenkins appeared beside them.

" I made that bear run, didn't I, Dick ? I guess he'll never undertake to follow Pete Jenkins again."

" No, I guess not," replied Dingle, gravely. " What made you holler so ?"

" What made me holler so?" asked Jenkins, indignantly. " Why, s'posen I hadn't let you know he was coming, what do you s'pose would have become of you ? He might have killed you both !"

" Where did you come across him ?"

" Why, I was walking back in the path, my head down, looking for danger, when I heard a grunt, and, looking up, seen the bear coming right straight at me. I drawed my toe across the path, and told him to put his paws on that mark, stand his ground like a man, and take the consequences on his head. But he come right over the mark, for all I shouted to him he wasn't acting fair, and I got so tearing mad that I—I—that I *left*."

" Why didn't you stand yer own ground, even if he didn't do the fair thing ?"

" Well, the truth, Dick, was—was I felt one of them *fainting-fits*—what you grinning at ? I felt one of them *fainting-fits* coming on !"

" I heard you bawl out something about Shawnees, Injins, and such things. What was that for ?"

" 'Pears to me, Dick, you hain't got common sense. You're getting worse and worse every day. If you had listened to my words, you would have heard me telling the bear that neither Shawnees, Indians, nor any one else would act in the outrageous manner he did. I shouldn't wonder, Dick, if you got to be a fool one of these days."

" I hope not," replied the trail-hunter, with an appearance

of meekness, "but Monowano looks as though he would like
to be on the move, and no doubt Miss Maude is 'just as
willin'; so let's be off."

When they reached Maude, the Indian said:

"Follow me," and took a direction at right angles from the
one they had hitherto pursued. Dingle concluded it prudent
to gratify him, and accordingly did as requested. A few
rods brought them to the river, where his object was soon
made known. Going a short distance down the stream, he
pulled forth a small canoe from some bushes and launched it.
Our friends stepped in it immediately and their united weight
sunk it to the very gunwales. Monowano seized the long
paddle and shot the frail vessel forward with amazing
swiftness.

Nothing further worth relating occurred upon their journey.
In due time they reached the settlement, where, as may be
supposed, their appearance created a great sensation. Dingle,
the instant he landed, stated his suspicions regarding Monowano to the commander of the block-house, who had him
instantly secured and confined in the strong room, where,
under guard, there was not the remotest possibility of his
escaping. When arrested, the Indian gave a start, and was
about to speak, but he checked himself and submitted quietly
to those that led him away.

Maude was instantly taken in charge by her numerous
friends, who attended her physical comforts, while they sought
to soothe her by holding out hopes regarding Mordaunt and
his men, and by concealing from her the fact that Monowano
had been arrested and would probably suffer death on their
account. Jenkins was in his glory. Had his listeners been
credulous enough to believe one half of what he told, they
would have imagined him the greatest hero the world ever
produced. He gathered crowds around him, and in his glowing narrations seemed to have forgotten entirely the existence
of such a person as Dick Dingle. Every thing had been done
by his own unaided arm.

The most influential men of the settlement met in the block-
house, on the following evening, for the purpose of coming to
some conclusion regarding Monowano. The conviction that
he was a spy had so gained ground that his death was

regarded as a foregone conclusion. It was in the hope of clearing up the mystery that hung around him, and to prevent any undue haste in so important a matter, that this gathering was called.

To give a parliamentary character to the proceedings, the commander of the block-house was chosen to preside. He stated the reason of thus collecting together, and called on Dick Dingle to relate what he knew of the person called Monowano, and the cause he had for believing him an enemy and a spy. The trail-hunter did so in a brief and straight-forward manner. He said he had never seen him previous to his appearance in the village somewhat over a year ago. He always had had a dislike to the "Injins," but he was favorably struck with this one. He failed to resemble a savage in many respects, and this had given rise to the many conjectures regarding his nativity. He turned his toes out in walking, and had not the features of an Indian. Dingle stated his belief to be that he was a half-breed. As the trail-hunter uttered the last two words, his listeners noticed he started and exhibited unusual agitation. He recovered, however, in a moment, and proceeded to give an account of the manner in which Monowano had dogged their footsteps when marching under Captain Whitley, and how he himself had cautioned him of the risk he ran in doing so. Dingle omitted nothing that he could say for or against him. When he came to narrate the dying words of Hickman, where he gave an account of the scalps he saw in possession of the Indians, while reconnoitering their position with a companion, the silence of his auditors was profound, and a skillful reader of human nature could have seen in the face of every one the settled conviction of Monowano's guilt. Dingle wound up by stating that he had promised Hickman, just before he died, to see that the spy's face had a good scrubbing, so as to settle the matter about his blood.

"That's all I've got to say, except that I've always had a likin' to him. The fust time I laid eyes on his picter, I took him to be an Injin I could like. We seemed to take to each other right off, and you all know, boys, how I've always stuck up for him : but 'tain't no use any longer. He's a gone coon, 'at's cl'ar."

Dingle having finished, Jenkins was called on to state what he knew. It was very soon evident that he knew too much, altogether. Some of his yarns regarding Monowano were so improbable that the laughter of his listeners could not be restrained. His whole aim was to make an impression regarding himself, and he accomplished it most successfully. When told rather peremptorily by the commander to "shut up," he did so by saying:

"I don't happen to know any thing more than anybody else about Monowano, and never expect to, except that he is a white man, an Injin, or a half-breed, particularly the last named, though I shouldn't wonder if he is one of the other, or both."

Russell Mansfield and Jim Peterson, being known to all as the warm friends of the accused man, were asked whether they had any reasons for his non-conviction. Both stated that they could give no *reason*, although their *feelings* revolted against his execution. Both now were well satisfied he was guilty, and had no wish to stand in the way of justice. As a jury was about being appointed, Dingle proposed that Monowano should be brought into their presence and questioned. This meeting with general favor, the commander directed Dingle and Peterson to bring him in.

In a few moments, Monowano appeared walking between them, but perfectly free. He proceeded with a stately and dignified step until he was opposite the presiding officer, when he turned and calmly confronted the numerous eyes turned toward him. His long, dark hair was loose, and hung over his shoulders, and his mantle was gathered in front by his folded arms.

"Monowano," said the commander, "at the request of the persons you see, you are brought hither. You are aware that you are accused of a great crime—one whose punishment *is death*. Your accusers are well known to you, and you must admit that their actions have not been incited by prejudice. On the contrary, some have contended up to this point for you, and against reason, as they are now free to confess. You are accused of being a spy, and a participant in the murder of Mordaunt's party—"

"Is he dead?" asked the prisoner, with a start, and speaking as quick as lightning.

"There is no evidence to show that he is alive, while the most incontrovertible evidence appears that not only he but all his men were massacred by the party to which you belonged. In the first place, Monowano, Hickman, the friend of us all, another victim to savage fury, *saw a number of scalps in their possession.* Above all, the suspicions which, previous to this sad affair, had been entertained against you, have never been explained. When asked to do so, you have refused. The best manner in which you can serve yourself, just now, will be to enlighten us in regard to yourself—where you came from, what your intentions have been, and who you chance to be."

The commander, when he had finished speaking, seated himself, as if to invite the accused man to vindicate. The latter, however, remained quietly surveying those present without saying a word. At length, Dingle, losing all patience, stepped a foot or two toward him, and asked:

"Are you an Indian, Monowano?"

The man, turning his gleaming eyes upon his questioner, looked at him as if he would pierce him through and through. Nothing but the deep, anxious breathing of the listeners could be heard during these few seconds, and the respiration seemed actually suspended, as he replied

"No!"

"What are you, then?"

"*A half-breed!*"

"Are you a spy?"

"No!"

"What is your business?"

"I am the friend of the white man."

"But how are you goin' to prove that?"

"If my deeds do not, then I must die."

"Your deeds happen to prove the opposite," said the commander, rising and taking upon himself the duty of questioner. "How do you account for the absence of Mordaunt?"

"I warned him and his men to turn back, but they disobeyed. I did not see them afterward, and can not tell whether they are living or dead."

"Did you not help attack the other boat?"

"I did."

"What was your reason for so doing?"

"Their own good. I saved three of their number by doing it."

"Who were these three?"

"Mordaunt's own daughter, Hickman, and Caswell Britt."

"Caswell Britt? Where is he?"

"I know not," replied Monowano, looking around the room as though searching for him. "But he was not killed. I saw him dive and escape."

"If you produce him before us, Monowano, it will be a good argument for you, but otherwise it can avail you nothing. In regard to saving Hickman, although willing to admit your intentions may have been good, that matter must also be ruled out; as Hickman's dying words to Dingle were such as to show he had strong doubts relating to you. Maude Burland was under your charge, and several other Indians who had participated in the massacre of the men, when she was rescued by Dick Dingle, and consequently he can more properly claim that credit—"

"I reckon Peter Jenkins had some labor to perform in that terrible affray," called out that individual himself.

"Please remove that noisy character," said the commander.

Jenkins found himself tumbling toward the door, and in a twinkling was shuffled out of it, his ejectors not pausing to hear the words,

"Remember what an awful retribution come upon Mordaunt for serving me such a trick, and see if you all ain't served as bad."

"Recollect, Monowano," said the commander, addressing himself to him again, "the circumstances were such as I have stated. How do you account for it."

The prisoner refused to reply.

"Have you any thing more to give?"

"Monowano has spoken."

"Remove him to his room then."

After he was gone, the commander said:

"Friends, it seems to me that in this matter of life and death you should proceed with due deliberation. It is plain that Monowano hopes to clear himself, but his manner has convinced me more than any thing else, that he is indeed guilty. But whoever are appointed to judge upon the matter, let them free themselves from prejudice, and give an impartial verdict."

Thereupon a jury was appointed, vested not only with the power of deciding upon a verdict, but with that of determining the punishment. This jury included Dingle, Peterson, and Mansfield, besides the requisite number necessary to make up the twelve.

Scarce ten minutes had elapsed after their appointment, when they made their appearance; and Mansfield, as speaker, said:

" We have consulted together, and find the prisoner, known as Monowano, to be a spy, and deserving of death. We there-fore decree that he be shot to-morrow, on the clearing, in front of the block-house at ten o' clock in the morning."

Some unimportant conversation occurred after this, when the settlers separated and returned to their homes.

The feeling existing, or which had existed, between Maude and Monowano was known to those who decided the fate of the latter, and this was the reason why it was determined he should be shot on the clearing, where it could not be wit-nessed by all. The matter was debated, and out of respect for her feelings, the commander enjoined upon them to keep the matter a secret with themselves as long as possible.

We will not look in upon Monowano during the night which he had every reason to believe would be his last upon earth. Those who guarded him stated that he walked the floor the entire night, and several times they overheard him muttering and communing with himself.

The troubled sleep of Maude Burland would have been a season of more agonizing, wrestling prayer had she known the awful fate which hung over her former lover, and whom she still regarded with affection, despite the dark doubts which hung around his name and deeds. But she was denied this second bitter cup.

At the appointed time, an assemblage numbering some fifty men appeared on the clearing mentioned. There were twelve men standing in a file, and holding loaded rifles, and others pacing off the ground and making every preparation for the dreadful execution.

Suddenly a **buzz of** surprise ran through them, as the minister appeared **conducting** Monowano. They could hardly believe the one whom they had all supposed to be an Indian, was the being before them. The deceptive paint was removed, and he was now a *white man*, with every characteristic of the European race. The dark hair, and faint, swarthy tinge of the cheek, only betrayed the Indian blood. That he was handsome and manly, all admitted ; and more than one heart bled that justice compelled them to sacrifice the life of such a remarkable man.

The crowd swayed back, and listened breathlessly as Dingle asked in a clear voice :

" Monowano, will you now tell us who you are ?"

The frame of the prisoner was seen to quiver with emotion, when, elevating his head, he said :

" *I am your son !*"

It would be vain for us to depict the sensation produced by this extraordinary reply. The trail-hunter started as if struck by a bullet ; the others pressed around as if insane with excitement. Gathering himself by a mighty effort, he moved forward, and laid his arm upon the prisoner's shoulder. Then gazing intently in his face a moment, he said :

" My son—the same eyes that his mother had—the same features—it was a long time ago that my little Willie was carried off—he looked like this one. Oh my boy ! why did you not tell me before ? To think your poor old father has been the means of havin' you shot."

The frightful paleness that overspread Dingle's face as he uttered these words induced Peterson to lead him away into the village, where the heart-broken man could not witness the execution of the only living relative he had on earth. During the confusion necessarily occasioned by this most wonderful revelation, Mansfield stepped up to the commander and said :

" My dear sir, since the discovery of Monowano's identity, can not his sentence be reversed ? William Dingle, the prisoner, is the only tie that binds his father to the world, and it certainly can not be the wish of any one here to strike down a man who has spent years entirely devoted to the welfare of our village. What cause has led the son to conceal his true character, I can not divine ; but, surely, we to whom mercy has been so bountifully accorded by the Supreme Being, can not refuse mercy in turn. I therefore ask that the prisoner be acquitted."

"Russell Mansfield," said the commander, with severity, and yet not without some feeling, "you decreed that that man should die, and at this point I can not persuade myself that your decision was formed from any prejudice ; but, that the favor you ask of me is impossible, is plainly evident. You, Dingle and others decided that you had reason to pronounce this man a spy, and therefore too dangerous to be allowed to live. This revelation of his identity does not affect the *crime ;* he is as much a spy this minute as he ever was ; and, although no one can inflict this blow upon Dingle with greater pain than it gives me, still I must do my *duty.* The prisoner will accordingly be led to the place yonder, and my assistant will see that the men and every thing are ready."

"Monowano, before executing this terrible but just sentence upon you, you should know the crimes for which you are accused. Had you revealed yourself sooner, your fate might be different. I believe that every one present is convinced that you are not only a *spy,* but the main cause of the murder of Mr. Mordaunt and his party ; and, as an impartial jury have decided that you should suffer death, I can not take it upon me to reverse the verdict. Can you give us any reason for believing you not guilty of the murder of Mordaunt?"

"Let Mordaunt answer for himself. Yonder he comes!"

The prisoner pointed up the river as he spoke ; and, as every eye was turned, all beheld a boat far up the Ohio, and slowly nearing the settlement. At the distance, it was impossible to identify any of its inmates, but the confident assertion of the prisoner led to a suspension of proceedings until this could be determined.

The whole multitude, including the prisoner, under careful guard, flocked down to the river and impatiently awaited the arrival of the boat. It would be impossible for us to show their suspense and impatience. The only cool and unexcited person was young Dingle. The flashing of the ashen blades could be seen, as they were dipped and raised in the sunlight ;

but still the men seemed strangers. All at once, Jenkins, who was the most nervous in the multitude, sprung into the air with a wild yell, and swung his hat over his head.

"I knowed it was Mordaunt all the time! That's him steering! Don't you see him grinning? And there's Caswell Britt using the oars, too!"

Such was indeed the case; and, a few moments later, Mordaunt and every one of his men, including Britt, stepped upon shore, amid their friends. Before half had shaken hands with the leader, he asked the commander who the person under guard could be.

"He is Monowano, under sentence of death for being a spy, and for betraying you and your party into the hands of the Indians!"

Mordaunt sprung forward and grasped his hand.

"God bless you, Monowano. Under heaven, the lives of us all are owing to you. Are you accused of being a spy? Unloose him this moment, for a truer friend to us never breathed!"

A few words explained every thing. Mordaunt stated that shortly after their boats had separated, Monowano appeared beside him in the river, and stated that the sound of their rowing had been heard by a large party of Indians, who were at that moment searching the river for them in a large canoe. Under the guidance of Monowano they were conducted to the mouth of a small creek, which put in from the Ohio side. Just as they were entering it, they encountered the very canoe from which they were endeavoring to escape. A race for life instantly commenced. Monowano, who, up to this moment, had swam before them, sprung into the canoe, seized the helm, and Mordaunt grasped one of the oars. The darkness was so great that at ten yards distance their enemies were invisible. The impetus given to their own vessel for a few minutes, by their excessive fear, carried them quite a distance ahead, and Monowano suddenly sheered the boat under some overhanging bushes, and several yards up a brook, as it afterward proved. Here, at his advice, the men landed, and carried the boat to the river bank, where they embarked and set out on their return to the settlement, Mordaunt being now perfectly willing to return after what he had witnessed.

Monowano left them to befriend the other party, while they continued their way. They heard the faint discharge of guns during the night, and in the morning Caswell Britt appeared on shore and was taken on board. He gave an account of the attack, and stated that his life, and he believed that of one or two others, was saved by the skillful maneuvering of Monowano.

After Mordaunt had finished, William Dingle (as he shall now be called) stepped forward and gave his story. He related how, when his mother was killed, in his father's absence, he was carried off as prisoner and adopted into the Shawnee tribe. His mother was a Wyandot, but was tomahawked by her own relations for marrying a white man. He was reared in the same tent with Tecumseh, and when quite a boy, was compelled, under pain of torture and death, to take an oath that he would not reveal himself to the whites. He was painted, and adopted their costume, and was believed to be one of their most loyal subjects. His prepossessing address led them to propose that he should act as spy for them, and he accepted the proposal for purposes of mercy. He had never forgotten his parent nor his people, and he had studied to befriend them whenever it lay in his power. Compelled to keep up the semblance of faith to the Indians, he necessarily ran a great risk. But his skill carried him through, though it came nigh failing him at the last moment.

And there were other facts which came out in time, all of which proved the loyalty of the suspected spy to the whites. He stated that more than once he had been upon the point of revealing himself to his " White Father ;" but his oath prevented, until it could not be avoided longer.

It was not until two years later that William Dingle related to his wife (Maude Burland Dingle) how nigh he had come to being executed on the very clearing in front of their cabin. It was a cold, gloomy night without when he related it, in his light-hearted manner, and she shuddered with terror as he laughingly painted the scene. But the fire upon their hearth was cheerful, and, as he turned his eyes upon his radiant wife, and his smiling father, the old trail-hunter, who sat upon the opposite side of the fireplace, he said :

"But the time has passed, and all are now satisfied that Monowano is their friend."

Young Dingle retained some of the characteristics of his Indian life as long as he lived. Among them was his habit of often using figurative language in conversation, and of being reserved and dignified in company. He proved, in after life, his loyalty to the interests of the whites, by greater achievements than any we have referred to.

Dick Dingle, true to his promise, gave over his wandering life, now that he had found his son, and spent the remainder of his days in the family of the latter, where, as his grandchildren grew up around him, he diffused perpetual sunshine and cheerfulness by his eccentric and good-natured peculiarities. He lived to a ripe old age, and his memory is still cherished by hundreds that occupy the scene of his former exploits.

As for Pete Jenkins— Ah! what of him ?   *We shall see!*